NAZI MOONBASE

BY GRAEME DAVIS

ILLUSTRATIONS BY DARREN TAN

OSPREY PUBLISHING
Bloomsbury Publishing Plc

Kemp House, Chawley Park, Cumnor Hill, Oxford OX2 9PH, UK
29 Earlsfort Terrace, Dublin 2, Ireland
1385 Broadway, 5th Floor, New York, NY 10018, USA
Email: info@ospreypublishing.com
www.ospreypublishing.com

OSPREY is a trademark of Osprey Publishing Ltd

First published in Great Britain in 2016

© Osprey Publishing Ltd, 2016

Transferred to digital print on demand in 2022

All rights reserved. Apart from any fair dealing for the purpose of private study, research, criticism or review, as permitted under the Copyright, Designs and Patents Act, 1988, no part of this publication may be reproduced, stored in a retrieval system, or transmitted in any form or by any means, electronic, electrical, chemical, mechanical, optical, photocopying, recording or otherwise, without the prior written permission of the copyright owner. Inquiries should be addressed to the Publishers.

The Publisher has made every attempt to secure the appropriate permissions for material reproduced in this book. If there has been any oversight we will be happy to rectify the situation and written submission should be made to the Publishers. All uncredited images are assumed to be in the public domain.

A CIP catalog record for this book is available from the British Library

Print ISBN: 978 1 4728 1491 3
ePDF: 978 1 4728 1 4920
ePUB: 978 1 4728 1 493 7

Typeset in Adobe Garamond Pro, Bank Gothic, Conduit and American Typewriter
Originated by PDQ Media, Bungay, UK
Printed and bound by Intellicor Communications, USA

The Woodland Trust
Osprey Publishing supports the Woodland Trust, the UK's leading woodland conservation charity.

www.ospreypublishing.com
To find out more about our authors and books visit our website. Here you will find extracts, author interviews, details of forthcoming events and the option to sign-up for our newsletter.

Contents

Introduction	4
The Bifrost Protocol	6
The Nazi Space Program	17
The Base	34
Moonbase Projects	44
The Hunt for the Moonbase	56
Appendix: Timeline	72
Further Reading, Watching, and Gaming	77
Glossary	79

Introduction

As 1944 began, the writing was on the wall for Nazi Germany. In the east, Soviet forces were advancing steadily after the disasters of Stalingrad and Kursk. To the south, fighting in Italy continued to drain men and materiel. In the west, American bombers pounded German industry and British night raids set cities ablaze as the Atlantic Wall defenses braced for an inevitable invasion.

While Hitler continued to spout rhetoric and exhort his troops to fight for every inch of land, other Nazi commanders made their own plans for the survival of the Third Reich. Jet aircraft, ballistic missiles, and other *Wunderwaffen* (Wonder Weapons) could delay the end, but not prevent it. Research continued at a frantic pace, but Germany's atomic bomb program had yet to produce a new weapon and the projected *Amerikabomber* would be of little value without it. It was time to plan for the survival of the Reich after the fall of Germany.

As Berlin fell and many SS and Nazi Party leaders made their way to Argentina via the "rat lines" of the ODESSA network, the Nazi occult organization known as the Black Sun put a larger operation into place. Key personnel were smuggled out of Germany to a secret base in the Antarctic, codenamed Neuschwabenland. Commanded by *SS-Obergruppenführer* Hans Kammler, this facility continued work to develop advanced weapons and other technologies until it was discovered by the Americans in 1947. Although the US forces were driven off, Kammler knew that it was only a matter of time before they returned in greater strength. He gave the order to evacuate Neuschwabenland to an even more remote location: the surface of the Moon.

This book tells the story of the Nazi moonbase codenamed *Walhalla* and the project that created it, from the beginning of Nazi space research to the present day. The base is described in detail, along with the research projects that were transferred there from Earth. Also covered is the profound but largely undocumented effect that the existence of the *Walhalla* base has had on postwar history. From US and Soviet efforts to capture Nazi scientists, through the Cold War and the Space Race, to the abandonment of the *Apollo* project and the present-day unmanned exploration of the Solar System, the *Walhalla* base and the advanced technology it contains cast a huge shadow even today.

Identified as the site of the Nazi moonbase, the Aristarchus crater gives a clear view of the Earth while remaining in sunlight for most of the lunar day. (NASA)

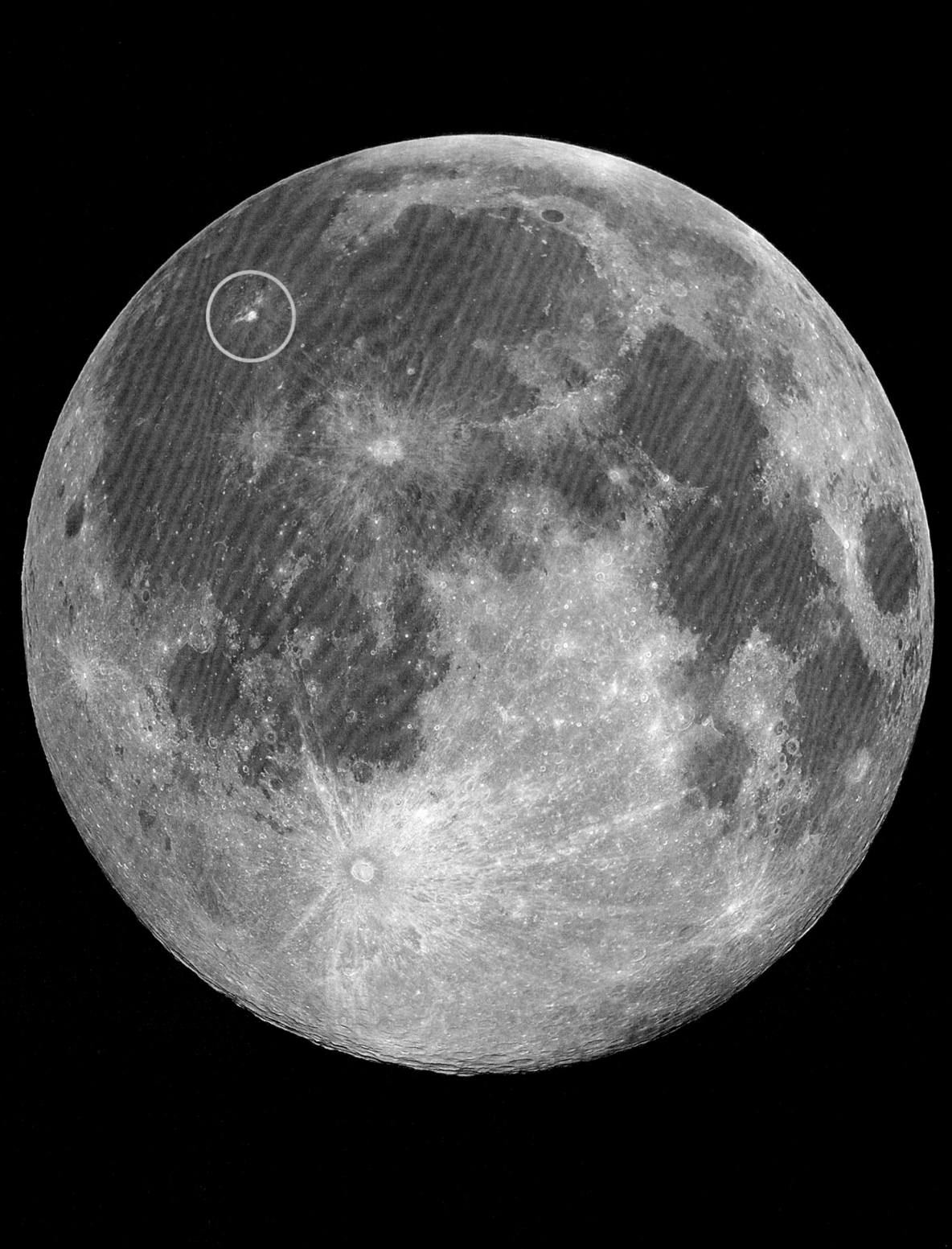

The Bifrost Protocol

The Nazi leadership knew by 1942 that *Wunderwaffen* offered Germany's only chance of winning the war. The *Blitzkrieg* had stalled, the Allies were preparing to fight back, and Germany had neither the men nor the resources to fight a protracted war.

Operation *Sea Lion*, the planned invasion of Britain, had been postponed indefinitely in September 1940, and the Luftwaffe's eight-month Blitz of late 1940 and early 1941 had failed to put Britain out of the war as Hitler had intended. The Royal Air Force continued to bomb German industrial targets, and the United States entered the war in December, raising the specter of countless American troops invading the Continent from southern England and turning the tide of the war, just as they had broken the stalemate of World War I in 1917.

Things were no better on the Eastern Front. Despite Hitler's rhetoric, Operation *Barbarossa* had failed to bring about the collapse of the Soviet Union. German forces had been thrown back 200 miles from the gates of Moscow, and the Red Army was rebuilding in the east. Unless a decisive blow could be struck, it was only a matter of time before Germany was crushed between the Western Allies and the Soviet Union.

The development of *Wunderwaffen* was given the highest priority. Several jet aircraft projects were already under way, including the Messerschmitt Me 262 fighter and the Arado Ar 234 bomber, but the Reich's greatest need would be for long-range weapons that could be launched from Europe to destroy targets as far away as North America and Siberia.

The first fruits of the *Wunderwaffen* initiative were the V-1 cruise missile and the V-2 ballistic missile, which entered service in June and September 1944 respectively. Resources were poured into the development of an atomic bomb: the *Amerikabomber* project and the A-9 rocket aimed to provide intercontinental-range delivery systems for nuclear warheads.

Other long-range bombardment initiatives sound like science fiction. The Oberth Sonnengewehr (Sun Gun) was a huge orbiting mirror designed to incinerate cities like ants under a magnifying glass. The V-3 supergun had a barrel 430 feet long and could fire a 150mm shell more than 100 miles.

As the tide of war turned against Germany, work on all these projects was hampered by Allied air raids and increasing material shortages. By March of 1945, even the most ardent Nazis knew Germany was doomed – but some dared to think beyond the defeat of Germany and make plans for the Reich to fight on and win eventual victory.

The Order of the Black Sun

Founded as an elite within an elite, the Order of the Black Sun had its origins at Heinrich Himmler's SS academy at Wewelsburg Castle in Westphalia. It took its name from a symbol on the floor of the *Obergruppenführersaal*, or Generals' Hall, which can still be seen there.

The symbol of the Black Sun was based on the design of brooches worn by the Germanic Allemani people during the post-Roman period. It resembles a sun emitting twelve jagged rays, and has been described as a triple swastika representing the sun at sunrise, noon, and sunset.

The Black Sun design represented a mystical power source and a design used by the medieval Germanic Alemanni. (Ratatosk under the Share Alike creative commons license)

Its origins in Nazi symbolism date back to the writings of Helena Blavatsky and Karl-Maria Willigut, two of several mystical writers of the 19th century who inspired various facets of Nazi occultism. More on this subject can be found in Kenneth Hite's *The Nazi Occult*, also in this series. The Black Sun represented a source of energy allegedly known to the ancient Aryans, which would shine over the rise of the New World Order.

Wewelsburg

In 1934, Heinrich Himmler rented Wewelsburg Castle from the local government of Westphalia for 100 years at the token rent of one mark per year, and set about refurbishing it as an SS academy and research institute. While it is true that certain chambers were renamed after characters from the Grail Romances, claims that Himmler intended Wewelsburg to be the new Grail Castle are exaggerated. However, he did envisage it as the functional and spiritual center of his new religion.

Himmler had long despised Christianity for its Jewish roots, and was in the process of formulating a Germanic faith for the Aryan race. Hitler expressed his opposition to the idea of *völkisch* religion and occultism as a part of National Socialism, both in *Mein Kampf* and in public speeches, but Himmler was determined that the SS – his state within a state – should have an ideology of its own, based on solid Germanic roots. The new religion would ensure that members of the SS would never feel torn between the principles of Christianity and Nazism.

Among its other functions, Wewelsburg was to be the center of this religion. After 1941, it was often referred to in documents as "the center of the world." While Hitler and his architect Albert Speer planned a new world capital in Berlin, Himmler planned Wewelsburg as a spiritual and intellectual capital.

OPPOSITE

Kammler was an ardent Nazi with a gift for organization which led him to the command of all *Wunderwaffen* production. (Artwork Hauke Kock)

The Rise of the Order

It was against this background that the Order of the Black Sun came together. Its members sought to combine science, politics, and mysticism into a single driving force that would underpin the new world order, and place themselves – as the masters of this new thinking – in effective control of the world.

Although Himmler maintained a mask of servility – Hitler nicknamed him *der treue Heinrich,* "loyal Heinrich" – by 1941 his ambition to succeed Hitler as Führer, and their differences over *völkisch* mysticism, led him to keep much of Wewelsburg's work secret. This work included the development of ideas and technologies that had originated within the Thule Society (*Thule Gesellschaft*) and the Vril Society (*Vril Gesellschaft*). The Thule Society had been disbanded on Hitler's orders in 1935, along with the Freemasons and other organizations, while the Vril Society was on the brink of a schism: its leading "Vril medium," a woman known to history only as Sigrun, insisted that its knowledge – especially the propulsion system used in the *Vril* series of saucer craft – should be used only for peaceful purposes. More information on both these societies will be found in the next chapter.

Even as Himmler began to distance Wewelsburg from Hitler, though, the Order began to distance itself from Himmler. Many leading members of the Order felt that Himmler's emphasis on the development of his Aryan religion was a distraction from the more urgent goal of developing the superscience, and superweapons, that would enable Germany to win the war; as the tide of the war began to turn, their frustration drove them to keep more and more from their former leader.

With Britain undefeated, the Soviet Union on the counterattack, and the United States poised to launch a European front, the Order looked for a way to save Germany – or if this was impossible, to ensure the survival of their work and plan for the creation of a new Aryan state. The man they chose to lead this effort was a rising SS star named Hans Kammler.

Hans Kammler

Hans Kammler was born in Stettin (now Szczecin, Poland) on August 26, 1901. At that time, Stettin was part of the German Reich ruled by Kaiser Wilhelm II. After World War I, he studied civil engineering in Danzig (now Gdansk) and Munich and was a member of the Rossbach *Freikorps*, a far-right paramilitary group whose members included a young Rudolf Hess. Kammler joined the Nazi Party in 1931 and the SS in 1933.

Kammler held various administrative posts in the Nazi government, starting as head of the building department in the Air Ministry (*Reichsluftfahrtministerium*). He joined the Waffen-SS in June 1941, and became Oswald Pohl's deputy at the SS Main Economic and Administrative Department (*SS-Wirtschafts-Verwaltungshauptamt*), whose duties included oversight of the concentration camp system.

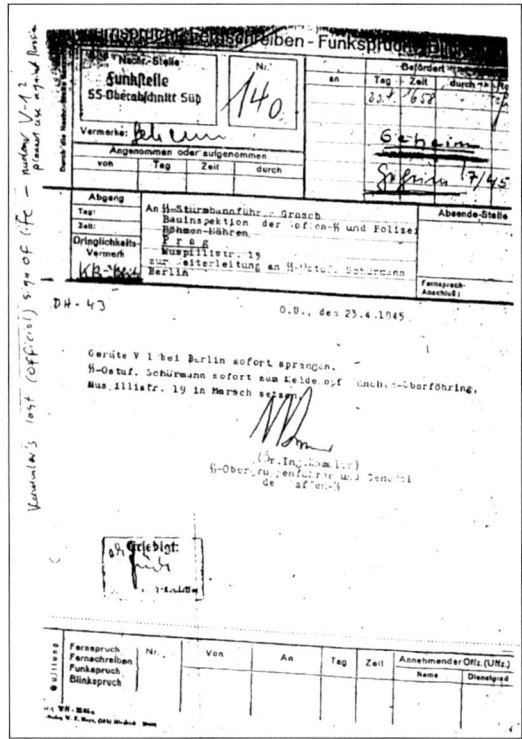

This memo ordering the destruction of a "V-1 device" (possibly a prototype of some kind rather than a V-1 flying bomb) is dated April 23, 1945 and bears Kammler's signature. It is the last trace of Kammler in Europe. (PD)

In 1942, Pohl assigned Kammler to construct facilities for various advanced weapons projects, including the Me 262 jet fighter and the V-2 ballistic missile. He rose quickly, largely thanks to his notorious expedient of using concentration camp prisoners as a source of slave labor. Hitler placed him in charge of all V-2 production, as well as transferring the responsibility for jet aircraft production from Hermann Goering to Kammler. On March 1, 1945, Kammler was promoted to the rank of *Obergruppenführer*, making him answerable only to SS chief Heinrich Himmler. A few weeks later, all special weapons development and manufacturing projects were absorbed into Kammler's SS Development Agency IV (*SS-Entwicklungstelle* IV, known as SS E-IV). Only Wernher von Braun's Peenemünde rocket group remained outside Kammler's control, and this only because of von Braun's obstinate refusal to acknowledge Kammler's authority. The conflict between Kammler and von Braun began as a simple clash of personalities, but came to have a profound effect on the history of manned space flight.

No one else in the Third Reich had such a comprehensive understanding of the new technologies being developed. As Germany crumbled, Kammler assembled a hand-picked team of scientists and devised a daring plan – to build a base on the Moon, bombard the Allied homelands with impunity, and return to Earth victorious once they had collapsed.

Officially, Hans Kammler committed suicide in May 1945, but the credibility of the supposed eyewitnesses has been challenged multiple times. The US Army Counterintelligence Corps (CIC) launched an unsuccessful hunt for him later in May. One former Office of Strategic Services agent claimed to have brought him to the United States, but this claim was never confirmed. By 1949, Kammler's name simply vanishes from intelligence documents, without any explanation.

Kammler's Plan

Kammler named his plan *Protokoll Bifrost* (The Bifrost Protocol) after the rainbow bridge of Norse myth that linked the mortal world of Midgard to the divine realm of Asgard. Simply put, it was a three-point plan to ensure Nazi survival – and eventual victory – after the fall of Germany. Its objectives were as follows:

Escape

The first priority was to ensure that all the necessary technology, personnel, and resources were placed out of the Allies' reach. In Kammler's original

SURGEON AND PAPERCLIP

In the months either side of the war's end in May 1945, Allied intelligence officers made a concerted effort to recover and turn German personnel who had been employed on advanced technology. Operation *Surgeon* was run by British Intelligence and Operation *Paperclip* by the US Office of Strategic Services. The latter's most notable success was the recruitment of Wernher von Braun and others of his Peenemünde rocket research group, who went on to play key roles in the American space program.

The stated purpose of both operations was to ensure that German advanced technology stayed out of Soviet hands: with the end of the war in sight, it was clear that the postwar world would be dominated by the rivalry between the capitalist West and the communist East.

The second, and perhaps more important, goal of these operations was known only to a few individuals in the very highest intelligence circles. From what Western intelligence agents had been able to discover about the Bifrost Protocol, it was clear that some Nazis had escaped and intended to fight on, using what MI6 chief Sir Stewart Menzies called "a continuation of the V-weapon offensive, conducted from some remote spot and using weapons of extremely long range with the goal of destroying the major cities of every Allied nation." The highest priority was given to uncovering more information about this planned offensive, and the recovery of any technology that could help thwart it.

documents, dated to early 1944, this phase of the operation was codenamed *Walküre* (Valkyrie), but it was renamed *Einherjar* after July 20, 1944, when a group of disaffected officers launched a failed attempt to assassinate Hitler under the codename *Walküre*.

In Norse myth, the *einherjar* were the warriors found worthy of admission to Valhalla. This was a perfect metaphor for Kammler's careful selection of projects and personnel, but it turned out to be too perfect. By now, Alan Turing's Bombe computer at Bletchley Park had cracked the German Enigma code, and MI6 quickly deduced that signal decrypts featuring the codename *Einherjar* referred to some Nazi effort to evacuate key personnel and technology from Germany. This intelligence resulted in the British launching Operation *Surgeon* and the Americans launching Operation *Paperclip*, which were intended to intercept and retrieve Nazi scientists and exploit their knowledge.

Bombardment

Once established on the Moon (codenamed *Walhalla*), the second phase of the Bifrost Protocol would begin. This phase, codenamed *Mjölnir* after Thor's mighty hammer, would see the development of *Wunderwaffen* capable of bombarding Earth and wiping out entire cities. This armament would be used to destroy the major cities belonging to the principal Allied powers – the United States, the Soviet Union, Britain, and France – and leave them with neither the population nor the industrial capacity to resist the third phase of the operation.

Kammler acknowledged that this would be the most critical phase of the Bifrost Protocol. In particular, he was aware that the *Walhalla* base would be living on borrowed time. Once the Allies became aware of the *Walhalla* base's existence, they would surely devote all their vast scientific and manufacturing

OVERLEAF
The *Haunebu IV* saucer received its final fitting-out at the *Neuschwabenland* base. Barely airworthy in mid-1945, it managed to evade the Allied advance and limp to Antarctica. This giant craft was to form the core of the moonbase.

11

resources to the task of developing weapons that could reach it and destroy it. *Mjölnir* would have to achieve its objectives before they could do so.

Return

The final phase of the Bifrost Protocol was codenamed *Gungnir* after Odin's deadly spear. With the Allied powers on their knees, the personnel of *Walhalla* would return to Earth as conquerors, raise up the fallen German nation, and establish an eternal Fourth Reich built upon the principles of the Third.

Antarctica

By March 1945, the Western Allies had crossed the Rhine and the Red Army was pushing westward from Vienna. Kammler knew that the first phase of the Bifrost Protocol had to be put into effect soon, but there was a problem: the massive *Haunebu IV* saucer, whose carrying capacity was vital to the evacuation plan, was not yet spaceworthy. With his characteristic efficiency, however, Kammler had foreseen this possibility and formulated a contingency plan.

The German Antarctic Expedition of 1938 had laid claim to a vast amount of territory on the continent of Antarctica, naming the territory Neuschwabenland (New Suebia) after one of Germany's ancient duchies. Although the Allies had ignored the Neuschwabenland territory, Kammler had not. In the closing months of the war, Kammler used the *Haunebu* craft, along with a fleet of U-boats, to move SS E-IV assets to Neuschwabenland.

The *Haunebu IV* limped out of Prague ahead of the Soviet advance, reaching Antarctica a few hours later after a flight beset with minor technical problems. When Kammler made the decision to take off, chief saucer engineer Klaus Habermohl was in the city scrounging for materials: he was captured by the Red Army on May 11, showing just how close the Russians came to capturing the craft itself and thwarting Kammler's whole plan.

Through 1946, Kammler and his remaining followers worked to develop the Antarctic base into a working development and manufacturing facility which would enable them to continue the war. While the *Haunebu IV* completed its fitting-out, work continued on various other advanced weapons projects as materials and facilities permitted.

Operation *High Jump*

Part of Kammler's plan was to liquidate his rival von Braun and transfer the Peenemünde rocket group to Antarctica along with his other projects, but von Braun was able to escape Kammler's trap and surrendered to the advancing American forces. It was during his debriefing by American intelligence that he first mentioned Kammler's plan and the secret base in Antarctica, but it was almost a year before he was believed.

In late December 1946, US Navy Task Force 68 converged on Neuschwabenland from three directions. Commanded by Rear Admiral

Artist's impression of the air battle in February 1947 which prompted the execution of the Bifrost Protocol. Although the American task force was repulsed, it was clear that the Antarctic base was not secure. (Artwork by Darren Tan)

Richard E. Byrd, Operation *High Jump* was a secret mission with the cover of establishing an American research base: with the Cold War just beginning and the Soviet Union using captured German scientists in its race to match America's nuclear capability, Washington did not want to alert the Kremlin to the existence of yet more Nazi *Wunderwaffen* and spark a war for control of Antarctica.

After a series of skirmishes in the waters around Antarctica, a force of *Haunebu* craft attacked Task Force 68. All of Byrd's aircraft were destroyed and several ships were damaged, but none of the saucers mounted heavy-enough weapons to destroy a surface ship. Seventeen days after the fight began, Byrd withdrew on February 23, 1947, but Operation *High Jump* had

In the closing months of the war, *Haunebu* saucers and U-boats were used to transfer personnel and materials to the *Neuschwabenland* base in the Antarctic: a staging post where final preparations were made for the journey to the moon. (MasPiz / Alamy Stock Photo)

proved that Neuschwabenland was vulnerable and Kammler knew that the Americans would return in greater force. His followers worked through the brutal Antarctic winter to complete the giant saucer, and at some time between March and November of 1947, Operation *Einherjar* was put into effect: all the personnel and assets at Point 211, as US Intelligence had codenamed the base, were removed to the Moon, and Neuschwabenland was abandoned.

Operation *Windmill*

It was December before another American expedition reached Antarctica. Codenamed Operation *Windmill*, it was ostensibly a geographical survey and training mission and a step toward keeping the previous expedition's "Little America" base open permanently. Under cover of this mission, the personnel of Operation *Windmill* searched for the Neuschwabenland base.

An extensive area was surveyed using three helicopters and an amphibious airplane, while a Marine Corps detachment equipped with tracked all-terrain M29 "Weasel" vehicles stood at the ready. The abandoned base was discovered on January 3, 1948, but bad weather delayed investigation for several days. By February 16 it was evident that the Nazis had abandoned Point 211, taking their saucers with them. The task force was recalled, and Operation *Windmill* was over.

The Nazi Space Program

German scientists were exploring the possibility of space travel long before war broke out, and science fiction had as strong an appeal in Germany as it did in the United States.

In 1925 – two years before Fritz Lang's seminal *Metropolis* and nine years before the first *Flash Gordon* comic strip – a film titled *Wunder Der Schöpfung* (Wonders of Creation) showed a German scientific team traveling through the universe in a spacecraft that served as the symbol of progress and an age of new technologies; it included the stirring slogan "Now Germany belongs to us, tomorrow the whole solar system." The film was a huge hit on its first release, perhaps because it promised a brighter tomorrow for the dispirited German people after the humiliating defeat of the Great War.

German youths – including the young Wernher von Braun – were avid readers of books like *Das Problem der Befahrung des Weltraums – der Raketen-Motor* (The Problem of Space Travel – the Rocket Motor) and *Die Rakete* (The Rocket), a magazine published by the Society for Space Travel (*VereinfürRaumschiffahrt*), and German engineers experimented with rockets and other propulsion systems.

Alongside the pioneering rocket work of Wernher von Braun and others, the Order of the Black Sun worked to develop the theories of the Thule Society and the Vril Society to create another kind of craft entirely: disk-shaped, with speed and acceleration that defied conventional physics, and powered by motors whose revolutionary design blended science and mysticism according to Black Sun principles.

The V-2 rocket was the only development of the *Aggregat* project that saw service in the war. Larger intercontinental missiles were planned but never produced. (PD)

WERNHER VON BRAUN

Born Wernher Magnus Maximilian, Freiherr von Braun in Wirsitz, Prussia (now Wyrzysk, Poland), von Braun could trace his ancestry through both parents to European royalty. He developed a passion for astronomy after receiving a telescope as a gift, and he was arrested at the age of 12 for causing a disturbance after fitting rockets to a toy car and sending it hurtling down a public street.

Undeterred, von Braun studied physics and mathematics in order to pursue his interest in rocket engineering, and in 1932 he earned a Bachelor's degree in mechanical engineering from Berlin's Technical High School (*Technische Hochschule*).

Although space travel remained his primary interest, he became involved in military rocket development. By his own account, he was a reluctant Nazi, joining the Party in 1939 and the SS in 1940 only after it became clear that this was the only way to continue his work in rocket science.

He became the technical director of Germany's rocket development facility at Peenemünde on the Baltic Sea, helping develop rocket engines and rocket-assisted takeoff apparatus for aircraft as well as the *Aggregat* rocket series that led to the development of the V-2 ballistic missile.

Along with his brother Magnus, von Braun surrendered to American forces on May 2, 1945. He was taken to the United States and became a leading light in NASA's rocket program, culminating in the *Apollo* Moon landings. Some doubt the sincerity of his claim that he worked for the Nazis reluctantly: it was routine for Operation *Paperclip* to "clean up" the records of imported German scientists to make them more acceptable.

While von Braun's rockets laid the foundations of both US and Soviet space flight, it was the saucers that became the vital component of the Bifrost Protocol – and of the *Walhalla* moonbase itself.

Nazi Rocket Research

The initial impetus for the Third Reich's space program developed out of the *Amerikabomber* project.

The *Amerikabomber* Project

Soon after the United States entered the war, the Reich Air Ministry issued a requirement for a long-range heavy bomber capable of striking the continental United States from bases in Europe, some 3,600 miles away, with the atomic weapons Germany was racing to develop.

Despite design submissions from every major aircraft manufacturer in Germany, the *Amerikabomber* project yielded little more than a handful of prototypes. Material shortages, Allied bombing of Germany's heavy industry, and the rapid advance of Allied and Soviet troops into Germany rendered the project unfeasible, and almost all available resources went toward the defense of the Fatherland.

The Sänger *Silbervogel*

Co-designed by Austrian engineer Eugen Sänger and his wife, mathematician Irene Bredt, the *Silbervogel* (Silver Bird) was a rocket-powered bomber designed to fly at about 3,100mph, or a little over Mach 4. Launched from a rocket sled and lifted to a suborbital altitude of 90 miles (475,000 feet), the plane would skip off the denser upper layers of the stratosphere like a stone across a pond, delivering a payload of up to 8,800 pounds – about 10 percent smaller than the bomb dropped on Hiroshima – before descending across the Pacific Ocean to land in friendly Japanese territory.

In 1942, the Sängers' design was considered too radical, and the Air Ministry focused on more conventional aircraft designs from established manufacturers including Messerschmitt, Heinkel, and Junkers.

The *Aggregat* Series

Based at Peenemünde on Germany's Baltic coast, the Army Research Center (*Heeresversuchsanstalt*) had been developing ballistic missiles since the early 1930s under the leadership of Wernher von Braun.

Their *Aggregat* series included the A4, which developed into the dreaded V-2 rocket. As the *Aggregat* program continued, the Center explored features like recovery parachutes, wings, and hybrid rocket-ramjet designs. The A9/A10 *Amerikarakete* (America Rocket) was a two-stage missile intended to render the *Amerikabomber* program unnecessary, and the A12 was a four-stage orbital rocket designed to take payloads of up to 22,000 pounds into low Earth orbit.

Rocket scientist Wernher von Braun surrendered to American troops after escaping a murder attempt by his rival Hans Kammler. Officially "cleansed" of his Nazi past, he went on to become a major figure in the American space program. (PD)

Kammler vs von Braun

After Kammler assumed control of all secret weapons production, he found himself increasingly in conflict with von Braun, who fought his efforts to absorb the Peenemünde rocket group into Kammler's own SS E-IV. Braun resisted fiercely, though his reasons for doing so are still debated. According to the statement von Braun gave to officers of Operation *Paperclip* after his surrender, he was a reluctant Nazi who only joined the SS when it became clear he would be replaced if he did not, and who objected deeply to Kammler's use of concentration camp prisoners as slave labor.

Documents captured from SS E-IV, on the other hand, paint von Braun as snobbish, abrasive, and highly territorial, hinting that the blue-blooded Prussian von Braun regarded the ardent Nazi Kammler as an upstart political appointee rather than a fellow scientist. Kammler's background was in construction and civil engineering, whereas von Braun had been studying rocketry since his youth; he was happy for Kammler to attend to the day-to-day problems of manufacturing weapons based on von Braun's designs, but he deeply resented Kammler's interference with the research and development process.

Von Braun was also dismissive of the *Amerikabomber* project and the various saucer initiatives, maintaining that long-range ballistic missiles offered a cheaper and more practical means of bombarding enemy cities and a firmer foundation for space travel. He regarded Kammler's other projects as a waste of resources – or, worse, a theft of resources from his rocket group – and was not afraid to say so.

This rivalry between von Braun and Kammler was to have a profound effect not only on the development of the *Walhalla* moonbase, but also on postwar space research and the shape of the Cold War.

Early Saucer Craft

While von Braun's rocket group continued their work along purely conventional lines, German saucer craft were inspired by more esoteric knowledge. In its early years, Nazism was influenced by several mystical groups, including the Thule Society and the Vril Society.

The Thule Society

Originally the Study Group for Germanic Antiquity (*Studiengruppe für germanisches Altertum*), the Thule Society was founded in 1918 and named after a northern country from Greek mythology. It has been claimed that a young Rudolf Hess was a member, along with other leading Nazis. The Society's research combined history, archeology, and occultism, and was instrumental in developing the idea of an ancient Aryan race with superhuman abilities. It dedicated itself to recovering the lost knowledge of the Aryans, and flying saucer technology was among the fruits of this effort.

From 1920 onward, Hitler took steps to distance the growing National Socialist German Workers' Party (*Nationalsozialistische Deutsche Arbeiterpartei*) from occult and mystical groups, including the Thule Society. The Society was officially suppressed, but continued its work in secret with the aid of powerful supporters within the Nazi Party. Without its knowledge, it is unlikely that the Nazi space program could have existed.

The Vril Society

In his 1871 novel *The Coming Race*, English author Edward Bulwer-Lytton described a subterranean master race whose power was based on a mysterious energy named *vril*. Although his work was fiction, it was embraced by leading Theosophist Helena Blavatsky and by several other occultists whose work would help shape Nazi ideology and mysticism.

VRIL DISK FIGHTERS

The *Vril-1-Jäger* (Vril-1 Fighter) was the first armed disk aircraft. Developed under the auspices of SS E-IV, it was 37 feet in diameter and was armed with two 30mm MK 108 cannon and two 7.92mm MG 17 machine guns. Early models had a solid metal dome, which was later replaced by a clear glass dome. While its top speed was reported as 7,456mph (or almost Mach 10), it could slow down for combat with conventional aircraft and execute 90-degree turns without subjecting its crew to excessive G-forces. Seventeen craft were built, and 84 test flights took place between 1941 and 1944.

The *Vril-2 Zerstörer* (Destroyer) was a heavy fighter concept that never left the drawing board: its advanced oval shape was too far ahead of its time. Little is known about the *Vril-3* through *Vril-6* craft, which may not have advanced beyond concepts or prototypes.

The *Vril-7 Geist* (Ghost) was spurred by the *Amerikabomber* project. It was 146 feet in diameter and carried a crew of 14. Arado built one prototype in 1944, but by now resources were being diverted to the *Haunebu* project (see below).

The *Vril-8 Odin* was the last *Vril* series design. The only prototype was in early testing when Berlin fell.

All of the *Vril* series craft were capable of space travel. According to captured Black Sun documents, further development of the series was aimed at developing a craft that could travel to Aldebaran, some 65 light years away, to make contact with the Aryans there. Among the designs on the drawing board at the war's end was the *Andromeda-Gerät* (Andromeda Device), a huge cigar-shaped spaceship capable of making the interstellar journey.

These same documents also record that the vril medium Sigrun was vocal in her opposition to the development of the *Vril* craft for military use. She vetoed Arado's request for a *Vril Triebwerk* drive to use in their E.555 *Amerikabomber* prototype, and clashed with Kammler repeatedly during the development of the *Vril* series saucers. It has been argued that this friction led directly to Kammler's patronage of the *Haunebu* project, which was under his sole control.

The Vril Society, named for this mystical energy that combined electromagnetism, gravity, and all the other forces of the universe, began as a splinter group within the Thule Society, but quickly took on a life of its own. It allegedly developed ties with Aleister Crowley's Order of the Golden Dawn in England, and with other occult groups around the world. Like the Thule Society, the Vril Society was suppressed as part of Hitler's move away from esoteric thought, but its work carried on in secret.

The Society's most significant work for the Nazi space program was a series of séances which claimed to make contact with an advanced Aryan civilization in the Aldebaran system, some 65 light years from Earth. In the course of these séances, vril mediums acquired vital information that enabled German engineers to create the advanced alloys and propulsion systems required for successful saucer development.

The Vril Society was revived some time in 1943 as the Black Sun began to pour resources into saucer research for the Bifrost Protocol. The process was not entirely smooth, however: several vril mediums maintained that saucer technology should only be used for peaceful space travel and opposed its military applications. Nevertheless, the Order of the Black Sun ignored objections and the development of armed saucer craft continued at an accelerated rate. Significantly, the *Vril* saucer series was discontinued at this point and succeeded by the *Haunebu* series, whose development was entirely under Black Sun control.

The Aryans of Aldebaran

The idea of the Aryan race began in the 19th century as a purely linguistic classification, but through the influence of Theosophy and other esoteric doctrines it became identified with a race of enlightened superhumans who lived in prehistoric times and whose diluted blood persisted in the Germans and other Nordic races of the 20th century. Much of Nazi racial policy was aimed at removing the "impurities" of other races from the German ethnic stock and breeding back to a pure Aryan strain – a "master race" that would rediscover its lost superhuman powers and take its place as the rightful rulers of the world.

The Thule Society was suppressed by the Nazi Party when they took power in 1933, but much of its thinking was shared by the Vril Society. As early as 1917, the German-Croatian medium Maria Orsitsch was conducting séances for the Vril Society and claiming to have made contact with an Aryan civilization living on a planet in the Aldebaran system, in the constellation of Taurus. Together with another medium called Sigrun, she relayed a series of documents in a secret Templar script and other languages, which are said to have formed the basis of all German saucer research.

The *Jenseitsflugmaschine*

The *Jenseitsflugmaschine* (Other-world Flight Machine) was the first German saucer craft. It was built in the summer of 1922; according to Thule Society documents the design was transmitted psychically to the vril medium Sigrun by Aryans who had been living in the Aldebaran system since 1919.

The craft's disk was made up of three stacked circular plates with a cylindrical motor running down the center of the assembly. When the motor was activated, the disks contra-rotated, creating a powerful electromagnetic field.

It is thought that the oscillating field was intended to open a wormhole to Aldebaran and place the machine's builders in direct contact with the advanced Aryan civilization there, but no such journey is documented. However, the surviving reports indicate that the *Jenseitsflugmaschine* demonstrated impressive flight characteristics, and Hitler authorized further development until 1934, when the craft was dismantled and taken to the Messerschmitt works in Augsburg for storage. The craft was almost certainly destroyed by American bombing, which devastated the site between February 1944 and February 1945.

The *Rundflugzeug* Project

Just as the *Jenseitsflugmaschine* was put into storage, a new disk aircraft was being tested at the Arado works in Brandenburg. The *Rundflugzeug* (Disk Aircraft) RFZ1 suffered a disastrous control failure on its first test flight in

June 1934. The craft was destroyed and the pilot barely escaped with his life, but the development of a more advanced RFZ2 was authorized.

The RFZ2 was 16 feet in diameter and had an improved vril drive with a magnetic-impulse steering unit. It was used for fast reconnaissance during the Battle of Britain, and its success led to the inception of the *Vril* project.

The BMW *Flügelrad*

While other saucer projects focused on advanced technologies, the BMW *Flügelrad* (Flying Wheel) prototypes were developed with more immediate goals in mind. Powered by jet engines and using a conventional disk-rotor, the *Flügelrad* was essentially a rotorcraft with a centrally-placed cabin, using the wash from the jet engines to drive the rotor.

Work began in 1943 and four prototypes were built. The early prototypes were pure disks, but later models had a tail added to improve lateral control. Despite its modest goals compared to the *Vril* and *Haunebu* programs, the *Flügelrad* project did not result in a flyable aircraft; ducting the jet wash through the lifting rotor caused control and stability problems that had not been overcome when the Red Army overran the Prag-Kbley testing facility.

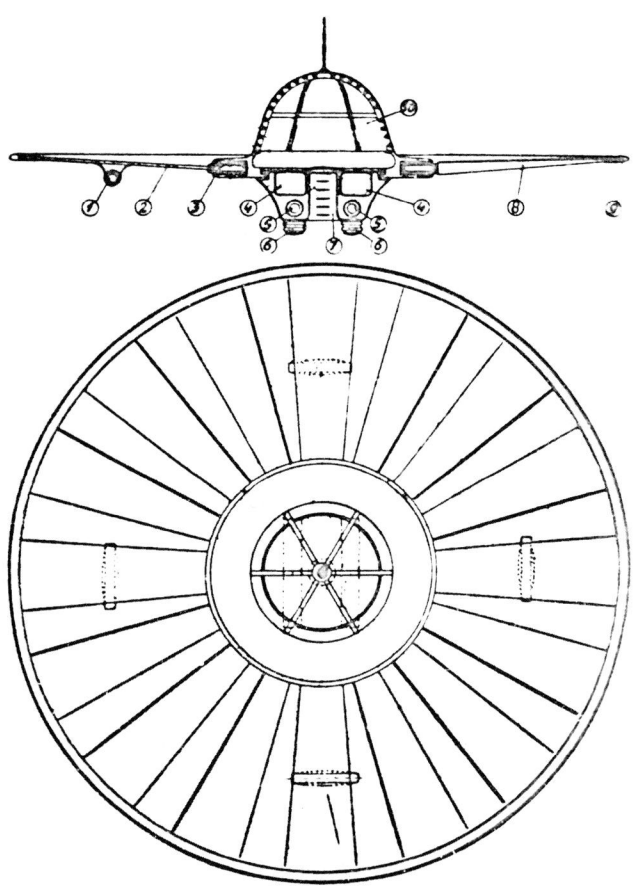

The BMW *Flügelrad* was essentially a jet-powered autogiro. It had some high-altitude potential, but control problems were never overcome. (INTERFOTO / Alamy Stock Photos)

The *Vril Triebwerk* Motor

Developed by the Vril Society from designs allegedly obtained psychically from the advanced Aryan civilization in the Aldebaran system, the *Vril Triebwerk* motor used contra-rotating metal disks studded with electromagnets which rotated at high speed. The interaction of their magnetic fields created an oscillation that was gradually intensified until it could warp space-time and create a wormhole to the desired destination.

While there is no documented proof that this was actually achieved, the electromagnetic-gravitic drive allowed a saucer craft to reach previously unheard-of speeds – up to Mach 10 according to some reports. The Triebwerk's gravitic warping also permitted a craft to change velocity and direction instantly, without subjecting the airframe or crew to G-forces that would be fatal under normal circumstances.

Test pilot Erwin Ziller wearing a *Dräger* pressure suit in the cockpit of a Ho-IX/Ho 229 flying wing, 1945. (Artwork Hauke Kock)

OPPOSITE
The moonbase under construction. Welders in modified *Dräger* pressure suits connect a *Haunebu III* to the base structure using tunnels made from pressurized bomber fuselages while saucers prepare to land. Note the triple-mounted KSK turret on the top of the saucer: the energy weapons were removed from the underside of the *Haunebu* craft before they were added to the structure, and moved to improvised top mounts for base defense.

The Haunebu Project

Working in occupied Prague, Rudolf Schriever and Klaus Habermohl developed a disk-shaped craft that consisted of a ring of turbine blades that rotated around a fixed central cockpit. The craft proved both fast and agile, and the Schriever-Habermohl project was quickly absorbed by SS E-IV. Under Kammler's personal direction a hand-picked team of engineers from all over the Reich worked to refine the airframe design and propulsion systems, and added a variety of armament including the *Feuerball* (Fireball) electrostatic weapon.

The resulting series of aircraft were given the name *Haunebu* or *Hauneburg-Gerät* (Hauneburg Device). Hauneburg was a wholly fictional name and did not refer to any place or person; it was coined simply to confuse and deceive Allied intelligence. There have been some claims that the project was moved to a remote testing-ground codenamed Hauneburg, but up to the time of writing not a single Nazi-era document has been recovered that uses the name Hauneburg as a place-name.

A breakthrough was achieved when the Shriever-Habermohl airframe was mated with a Thule-developed electromagnetic-gravitic propulsion system

Very little documentation on the *Haunebu* project survived the war. This typewritten page giving brief details on the *Haunebu II* craft is one of a handful recovered by Operation *Paperclip*. (PD)

named *Tachyonator-7*. Test flights using this drive recorded speeds of up to Mach 2 and a climb rate of almost 14,000 feet/minute – more than five times the climb rate of a Spitfire. Early tests also reached altitudes in excess of 40,700 feet, which was far beyond the reach of the best Allied aircraft.

Haunebu I

After the encouraging results of these early tests, Kammler authorized a full-scale development effort. The two *Haunebu I* prototypes were larger than the Shriever-Habermohl airframe and made of a specially-developed alloy codenamed *Victalen*. They were 81 feet in diameter – a little longer than a B-17 Flying Fortress – and according to some reports could reach speeds close to Mach 4.

For weapon tests, the second prototype was fitted with a turret mounting twin 60mm *Kraftstrahlkanone* (KSK) energy-beam weapons, but firing them caused a massive energy drain which led to stability problems and subsequent tests used two packs of three MK 108 30mm cannon, which was standard armament for many German fighters.

Haunebu II

At 85 feet diameter, the *Haunebu II* was only slightly larger than its predecessor and incorporated only minor improvements.

Testing between 1942 and 1944 led to the development of the *Haunebu II Do-Stra* (*Dornier Stratosphären Flugzeug*: Dornier Stratospheric Aircraft). Although it was classified as a development of the *Haunebu II*, the *Do-Stra* was effectively a different craft. The *Haunebu* II's Mach 5 performance was increased to a staggering Mach 17, and it was armed with seven pairs of *Kraftstrahlkanone*: three pairs of 80mm weapons turret-mounted on the craft's underside and a single 110mm KSK mounted above the cockpit.

This was the first *Haunebu* craft considered ready for large-scale manufacturing. Both Junkers and Dornier tendered for the contract in late 1944, and as the name suggests it was Dornier's bid that was accepted by the Air Ministry. However, Allied strategic bombing prevented Dornier from completing more than a handful of craft: the exact number is still unknown.

Haunebu III

The *Haunebu III* was a quantum leap from the *Do-Stra*. Nicknamed "Ostara" after an ancient Germanic goddess, it was three times the size of its predecessors and almost twice as fast. It also mounted a fearsome armament: no fewer than 22 KSKs between 50mm and 110mm, plus 60 MK 108 30mm cannon.

THE BATTLE OF LOS ANGELES

At 3.16 am on February 25, 1942, an unknown aircraft appeared in the skies over suburban Los Angeles. A photograph published in the next day's *Los Angeles Times* shows searchlight beams converging on a large circular object, and the 37th Coast Artillery Brigade reportedly fired more than 1,400 rounds at the unknown craft. Despite several reported direct hits, the craft moved off in the direction of Long Beach and was lost to view.

Within hours of the incident Secretary of the Navy Frank Knox held a press conference, saying the entire incident was a false alarm caused by anxiety and "war nerves." The US Government never explained the Battle of Los Angeles further, but UFOlogists have long claimed that the mystery craft was extraterrestrial in origin. However, it is interesting to note that the *Haunebu I* prototypes were already flying by early 1942, and the larger *Haunebu II* was under development.

This was the first *Haunebu* craft to be capable of space flight, and several writers have claimed that it was used for a suicide mission to Mars, taking selected personnel and equipment out of the reach of the advancing Allies in March 1945. While the evacuation did indeed take place, it was a far less desperate affair than these claims suggest: the Neuschwabenland base in Antarctica had already been prepared as a refuge and regrouping point.

With the burden of *Do-Stra* manufacturing taken on by Dornier, SS E-IV was able to complete multiple *Haunebu III* prototypes, while simultaneously designing and building the next craft in the series.

Haunebu IV

The final stage of *Haunebu* development – at least on Earth – was twice the size of the *Haunebu III* at 390 feet across, making it the largest heavier-than-air aircraft ever to have flown in Earth's atmosphere. Only one was constructed: barely airworthy when the Red Army advanced on Prague, it was able to limp to Antarctica for the final stages of fitting-out.

A *Haunebu III* craft prior to the Neuschwabenland evacuation. The provenance of this photograph is obscure, but it was most likely taken near Prague in March or April 1945. Note the *Kraftstrahlkanone* in the underside turrets. (Dale O'Dell / Alamy Stock Photo)

The *Feuerball* antiaircraft weapon led to the first reports of "foo fighters" by Allied pilots. (Mary Evans Picture Library / Alamy Stock Photos)

Advanced Aircraft Weapons

While early saucer craft were armed with the same guns as German fighters, Black Sun research soon provided Kammler with a new generation of energy-based weapons. Some problems arose from their power drain on the ships' propulsion systems, but these were eventually overcome.

Foo Fighters

From November 1944 onward, Allied pilots began to report strange flying objects and phenomena. Round objects, often glowing red, white, or orange, were seen following their aircraft and making sharp turns that seemed aerodynamically impossible. Named "foo fighters" by American aircrews (from a nonsense word in a popular comic strip), they were impossible to outmaneuver or shoot down, and they often seemed to be toying with the aircraft they encountered, zooming nearer and further as if taunting them.

Various explanations were advanced, including a new type of flak weapon and a natural electrostatic phenomenon like Saint Elmo's Fire or ball lightning, but none of the theories could account for the fact that the lights moved as if under intelligent control.

MK 108 Cannon

The *Maschinenkanone* (MK) 108 was a short-barreled 30mm cannon which became standard armament on most German fighters after 1943. Its predecessor, the MG/FF 20mm cannon, required around 20 hits to destroy a heavy bomber like the American B-17 Flying Fortress, which the MK 108 could accomplish in four.

Early *Vril* and *Haunebu* saucers were armed with MK 108s, mounted in packs of three, to supplement their energy-based weapons. However, the

MK 108 was less suited to saucers than it was to conventional airplanes. The main problem was targeting: the saucers moved so quickly relative to their targets that gunners would "lead" by too much or too little. Energy-beam weapons, on the other hand, fired at the speed of light and struck almost instantaneously, making targeting much easier.

Despite this, the MK 108 continued to be fitted to most German saucers as a secondary weapon. After some trial and error, it became a fairly effective defensive armament, used mainly when the massive energy drain of a KSK shot left the craft hanging in the air.

Although the saucers that formed the *Walhalla* base almost certainly took their MK 108 armament with them, it is uncertain whether this weapon could be effective in lunar conditions. A 1947 report in the archives of Britain's Ministry of Defence concludes that while the ammunition could be kept stable despite the wide temperature variation of a typical lunar day (-280 to +250 degrees Fahrenheit), there would still be some degradation in performance. The report also points out that the Moon's lack of an atmosphere would affect the gun's gas-operated mechanism to some extent. Be that as it may, after-action reports from attacks on the base have only mentioned its energy-beam weapons: the cannon do not seem ever to have been used.

Feuerball

The *Feuerball* (Fireball) was an experimental weapon, launched from the ground against Allied bomber streams. It was a small, unmanned disk aircraft, remote-controlled on takeoff and guided toward its target by sensors that tracked engine exhaust. It was fitted with an electrostatic field weapon developed at Messerschmitt's Oberammergau facility in Bavaria: burning chemicals produced a fiery halo around the craft, along with a powerful electrostatic field that could knock out a target aircraft's ignition systems causing total engine failure.

Normally deployed in groups of three to ten, the *Feuerball* weapons acted as a proof-of-concept for electrostatic weaponry, and led to further development. First deployed in November 1944 against RAF night attackers, the *Feuerball* saw service for barely two months before being replaced.

Kugelblitz

Not to be confused with the self-propelled antiaircraft gun of the same name, the *Kugelblitz* (Ball Lightning) was a larger version of the Feuerball's electrostatic weapon, which was fitted to several early saucers. Although *Kugelblitz*-equipped saucers did fly test missions against the American bomber streams, the program's main purpose was research and development. By the time the *Haunebu* saucers entered service, the electrostatic weapon concept had fallen out of favor. Future development of saucer armament focused on the more promising avenue of energy-beam weapons.

Rheotron

The Rheotron developed from a particle accelerator developed by Max Steenbeck at Siemens-Schuckert in the 1930s, similar to the Betatron developed by Donald Kerst at the University of Illinois in 1940. Both devices produced high-energy electron streams, but the German project was the first to weaponize the effect. By early 1945, SS E-IV had developed a vril-powered Rheotron small enough to be mounted in a large aircraft. Focused by a ring of electromagnets, the resulting energy beam was capable of melting aluminum in seconds.

The original Rheotron accelerator was captured by Patton's Third Army at Burggrub in western Bavaria on April 14, 1945. No aircraft-mounted versions were ever recovered, but Dr Rolf Widerøe of the Dresden Plasma Physics Laboratory confirmed their existence when he was questioned by US intelligence officers. According to Widerøe, he had demonstrated the Rheotron for Kammler several times, and provided copies of plans and notes to be used by the scientists of SS E-IV.

During the final months of the war, several B-17 bombers returned to their bases in England with unexplained damage, mainly in the wing and tail sections, after reported contact with "foo fighters." A classified US Air Force report likened the damage to "the effect of a hot wire on a block of cheese."

Röntgenkanone

The Rheotron was not the only energy-beam weapon developed under Kammler's patronage. Widerøe's rival Ernst Schiebold created the X-ray Cannon (*Röntgenkanone*), which produced a focused beam of hard X-rays. A prototype was used to disable the magnetos of Allied bombers and force them down to a lower altitude where they were more vulnerable to flak.

By powering a *Röntgenkanone* with the *Vril Triebwerk* motor, SS E-IV scientists were able to produce a weapon for the *Haunebu III* whose output was sufficient to burn out all electrical systems in an enemy aircraft. During Operation *High Jump*, personnel aboard the command ship USS *Mount Olympus* experienced severe radio and radar interference during the air battle of February 6, and both the *Mount Olympus* and several other ships were forced to undertake extensive repairs to their electrical systems before leaving Antarctica two and a half weeks later.

Kraftstrahlkanone

The *Kraftstrahlkanone* (KSK) has been incorrectly described as a laser weapon, but in fact it uses a focused energy beam. Power is channeled through spherical cascade oscillators to a transmission rod wrapped in a tungsten coil which acts as the "barrel" of the weapon.

The first KSK weapons were 60mm weapons tested in the *Haunebu I* prototypes, which projected an energy beam capable of penetrating 4 inches of conventional armor – more than an inch thicker than the frontal armor of a

A captured Ho 229 flying wing aircraft on its way to Area 51. American engineers learned more from German flying wing aircraft than from the fragmentary evidence of saucers. (PD)

Sherman tank and equal to that of the dreaded Tiger II. As part of the *Haunebu II* project, 80mm and 110mm versions were developed, with correspondingly higher performance. A smaller 50mm weapon was also developed as secondary armament for the *Haunebu IV*.

The KSK could have been a war-winning tank or aircraft weapon except for one thing: its extremely high energy demands. No conventional generator could power even the smallest KSK weapon, and with the *Glocke* (Bell) vril energy source still in development in 1945, only a very few KSKs could be mounted in fortified emplacements. In fact, Kammler issued an order in January 1945 recalling all available KSKs to keep them out of enemy hands. Only the *Haunebu* craft had the energy to power them and the mobility to avoid capture.

Continuing development of the *Vril Triebwerk* motor reduced the power drain problem, but it was not until the *Haunebu IV* was fitted with a small *Glocke* that it was eventually overcome. Only the *Glocke* could provide enough energy to fire the weapons without affecting flight functions.

Area 51

While von Braun and his fellow rocket scientists were shipped to New Castle Army Air Field near Wilmington, Delaware to continue the work that would result in the *Apollo* Moon rockets and America's arsenal of intercontinental ballistic missiles, another facility was set up at Groom Lake, deep in the Nevada desert.

Codenamed Area 51, this base was devoted to collecting and studying German advanced aircraft captured during the war. Among the captured aircraft sent there were Messerschmitt Me 262 jet fighters, an incomplete

Gotha Go 229 flying-wing jet bomber, and a handful of documents and parts recovered from the abandoned *Haunebu* facilities in the West.

Over the following decades, research at Area 51 produced a number of advanced designs based on German prototypes. The Northrop YB-49 flying-wing bomber was a straightforward development of the existing YB-35 design dating back to 1941, fitted with jet engines and incorporating several improvements based on the captured Gotha aircraft. Although the design never entered service, it is considered an early ancestor of the B-2 Spirit stealth bomber.

Several experiments with disk-shaped aircraft were less successful. Working from anecdotal accounts of Thule and *Haunebu* saucers and lacking reliable information on the Thule *Triebwerk* propulsion system, engineers at Area 51 tried to reproduce German saucer craft from first principles. The Vought XF5U "Flying Flapjack," developed from an earlier design by Charles H. Zimmerman, was a conventional aircraft with a disk-shaped wing rather than a true flying saucer. It was canceled in March 1947 due to disappointing performance.

Other disk designs were carefully kept out of the public eye – so carefully, in fact, that some commentators have claimed that the "Flying Flapjack" program was never intended as anything more than a smokescreen to explain sightings of disk-shaped aircraft over the continental United States from 1947 onward, leading to the great "saucer scare" of the late 1940s.

While some progress was made in replicating the *Victalen* alloy used in German saucer craft, the Americans encountered serious problems with propulsion and control. On June 24, 1947, pilot Kenneth Arnold saw a half-moon-shaped aircraft leading a formation of nine disks near Mount Rainier, Washington, and reported their flight as "like a saucer if you skip it across water." As the rumor spread that these craft came from another world, later UFO sighting reports of disk-shaped craft performing extreme maneuvers were generally attributed to advanced alien aeronautics rather than control problems.

"UFO" Crashes

On July 8, 1947, a small experimental disk aircraft crashed on a ranch outside Roswell, New Mexico. Eyewitness descriptions of the wreckage and the crew, and the military's efforts to suppress the incident, have combined to fuel an almost endless stream of conspiracy theories. Today, the incident is written off as the crash of a high-altitude balloon launched as part of Project Mogul, whose purpose was to detect Soviet nuclear tests using sound waves. In fact, the Roswell wreckage did come from a crashed saucer – but not from an alien spacecraft.

In an effort to understand and overcome the stability and control problems encountered by their experimental saucer aircraft, the engineers at Area 51 had constructed a series of scaled-down, radio-controlled craft. Some of these were "crewed" by rhesus monkeys – also used in the NASA rocket program – to study the effects of saucer flight on primate physiology. One such craft, with 16 monkeys on board, was shot down near Aztec, New Mexico in March 1948 after drifting over the Los Alamos National Laboratory: despite official attempts at a cover-up, the sight of their charred corpses led to rumors of "childlike" aliens which persisted for many years.

Sign, Grudge, and Blue Book

Following the saucer sightings of early 1947, the US Air Force was commissioned to produce a study of UFO reports for publication. The resulting Project Sign was active for most of 1948 before being shut down – allegedly for classifying too many reports as "unknown" – and replaced by Project Grudge, which sought to quash any theories about extraterrestrial origin. In August 1949, Project Grudge issued a 600-page report that concluded quite firmly that there was no such thing as flying saucers.

However, not everyone in the US military was satisfied with the Grudge report. In 1952 another study was commissioned under the name Project Blue Book. This ran until 1970, and remains the best-known official study of UFOs. Like its predecessor, though, Blue Book concluded that all of the 12,618 UFO reports it had studied could be explained by phenomena other than flying saucers.

Some of the Blue Book report is still redacted, allegedly to protect the identities of named witnesses. However, at least some of this material refers to incidents where saucers buzzed other aircraft, which were probably "hot dogging" test pilots exploring the limits of what even an American saucer craft could do. It is also noticeable that most of the early saucer sightings took place in southern California, Arizona, and Nevada – all within reach of the Area 51 facility. After American saucer research shut down, this type of sighting disappears from the record almost completely.

The famous "Silverman" photo actually shows the corpse of a rhesus monkey recovered from the crash of an experimental disk craft, probably at Aztec, New Mexico. The photograph was later played down as an April Fools' hoax. (PD)

The Base

The planning of *Einherjar* faced Kammler with many challenges. Given the hostility of the lunar environment, it was imperative that the *Walhalla* base should be designed for rapid – if not instant – construction, using only materials brought from Earth. It had to be placed in a location that gave it a clear view of Earth for the *Mjölnir* bombardment phase, but this location also had to be somewhat concealed, to protect the base from discovery and counterattack for as long as possible. If possible, too, there should be easy access to lunar minerals and other resources that would be needed for the planned scientific projects.

Moonbase Myths

For as long as people have been writing about the Nazi moonbase, there have been two enduring myths: that the base is on the dark side of the Moon, and that it is shaped like a swastika. Both are completely incorrect.

Symbolism aside, a swastika-shaped building is impractical, especially if personnel are restricted to the inside. It simply takes too long to move from the end of one arm to the end of another, and connecting passages rapidly become choked with traffic.

A base located on the dark side of the Moon is also impractical. While it is not literally dark, the far side of the Moon faces away from the Earth, making it impossible to observe – or fire upon – the Earth from a location there. Kammler and his followers needed to be able to keep a watch on the Earth, monitor radio transmissions, and aim their planned *Wunderwaffen* at the United States and other targets.

Location

Haunebu III scouts completed several survey missions in 1946 and 1947, while final preparations for *Einherjar* were under way at Neuschwabenland. Possible sites were examined around the edges of the Sea of Tranquility and in the mountain range south of the Ptolemaeus crater.

The site Kammler eventually chose was the Aristarchus crater, in the northwest of the Moon's near side. At 24.9 miles across and 2.3 miles deep, the crater allowed room for the planned base to grow while remaining small enough to be defensible in the event of an attack. The shadows of the crater's rim would help conceal the base from any Earth-based telescope then in existence. The nearby Aristarchus Plateau showed signs of volcanic origin, holding out the hope of much-needed metals and minerals.

Most important of all, though, was the crater's position on the Earth-facing side of the Moon. Aristarchus gives a good view of the Earth, but is sufficiently offset from the center of the near side to place the base in sunlight at most times. As well as providing vital warmth, sunlight was critical to one of the base's weapons, for which Kammler had high hopes during the bombardment phase.

Layout

When Kammler was planning the Bifrost Protocol and the construction of the *Walhalla* base, Germany's heavy industry was under considerable strain. American daylight raids were crippling Germany's industrial capacity, and the advancing Red Army was overrunning vital oilfields and mines, choking the supply of raw materials. As the SS head of *Wunderwaffen* production, Kammler had access to a wide range of existing projects, but he could not commission any special projects of his own. Therefore, he decided to design the *Walhalla* base around existing craft and structures, all of which could easily be transported to the Moon.

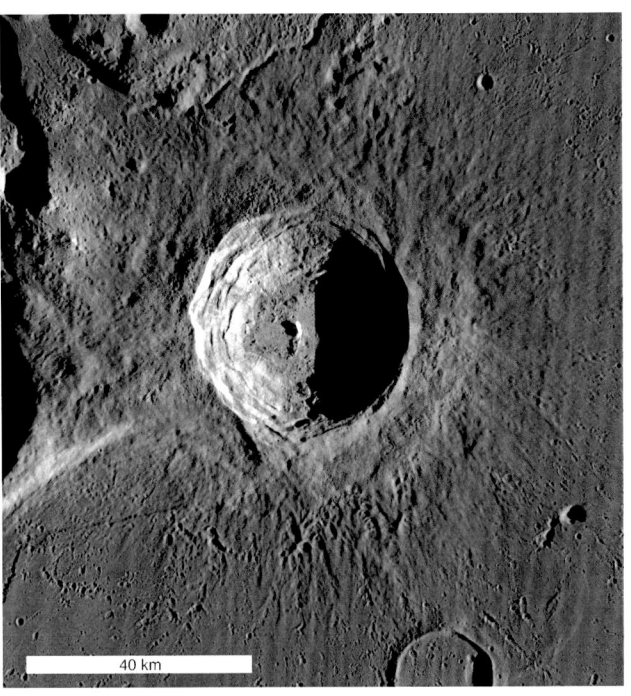

A close-up of the Aristarchus crater. The Nazi base is located on the right of the crater in the portion of the picture currently in shadow. (NASA)

The base was laid out using the escaped *Haunebu* fleet as primary structures. The huge *Haunebu IV* acts as the command center and provides accommodation for the base's personnel. The *Haunebu III* craft are laid out in a circle around it, connected by tunnels made up of the pressurized fuselage sections from Focke-Wulf Ta 400 high-altitude bombers.

Some commentators, unable to give up the romantic idea of a swastika ground-plan, have suggested that the layout of the *Walhalla* base is a form of the Black Sun emblem, but this is unlikely. Nothing in Kammler's history shows him to be anything other than a ruthless pragmatist, and the wheel-shaped layout is simply the most practical given the components on hand. It connects every part of the base in a way that minimizes distance and offers multiple routes between two points in case a particular tunnel should be damaged, blocked, or simply jammed with other traffic.

Accommodation

The *Haunebu IV* sits at the center of the base. The upper levels are devoted to command and communications, the middle levels to accommodation, and the lower levels to maintenance and logistics.

THE FOCKE-WULF TA 400

The Focke-Wulf Ta 400 was one of the contenders for the *Amerikabomber* project. Although the Messerschmitt Me 264 was the front-runner, Reich Air Ministry documents from 1944 and 1945 show that Kammler demanded unusually extensive manufacturing tests on the Ta 400's pressurized fuselage sections. Cabin pressurization allowed an aircraft to operate at higher altitudes, out of reach of all but the heaviest flak and the most advanced fighters, and Kammler claimed the test runs were necessary to perfect this new design feature, which would surely be useful even if the Ta 400 was not put into full production.

Under the pretense of his manufacturing tests, Kammler supplied himself with enough of the pressurized bomber fuselages to link all the *Haunebu* craft and turn the *Walhalla* base into a single structure.

The middle levels of the *Haunebu IV* were originally designed as a series of bomb bays to carry the nuclear and other weapons that the craft was designed to drop on the continental United States. As part of the craft's final fitting-out in Antarctica, the bay doors were sealed shut and the space converted to a series of bunkrooms and cabins some four stories high.

The *Haunebu* IV's Thule *Triebwerk* 9b power source is located in the lower levels of the craft, along with SM-Schweber maneuvering motors and associated equipment and couplings. After landing the underside weapon positions were stripped and their weapons moved to upper mountings: this created space for a series of maintenance workshops and supply stores. These levels are also hard-sealed to the underground storage bays and mineral processing plant that were excavated underneath the craft.

Laboratories

After landing, the *Haunebu III* craft were adapted for use as laboratories and workshops. In addition to food production and waste processing functions, they house several E-IV branches devoted to weapon development, genetic engineering, and other research, which are described in a later chapter.

Construction

The initial phase of construction was necessarily brief. The smaller saucers lifted the fuselage-passages into place around the *Haunebu IV* before landing themselves, and welding crews connected the base together, working both inside the base and outside on the lunar surface. After initial pressurization, smoke was used to detect flaws and leaks, which were patched from the outside. A *Glocke* vril generator was brought from Neuschwabenland to power the base, and air recyclers from Type XXVI U-boats were adapted to provide basic life support.

As the base expanded, underground chambers were dug using vril power, and mineral extraction sites were set up both beneath the base and out on the Aristarchus Plateau. Pressure bulkheads were added to the *Haunebu* craft, creating a hard seal with the lunar bedrock, and the excavated chambers

Artist's impression of the Ta-400. The pressurized fuselage sections were used as connecting tunnels, running between the *Haunebu* craft that formed the main structures of the base. (Artwork Hauke Kock)

were sealed using a compound called *Klebstoff X*, which had been developed as an adhesive to speed construction of aircraft and U-boats. By 1972, it was estimated that as much as 75 percent of the *Walhalla* base was located underground.

The *Dräger* Pressure Suit

Any activity on the lunar surface requires a pressure suit. During the first phase of construction, *Walhalla*'s crew used a modified version of the *Dräger* suit, which had been developed for high-altitude aircraft such as the Horten Ho 229.

Based on the diving suits which were Dräger's main product, it was made of laminated silk and rubber with a helmet made of a clear rigid plastic. It performed reasonably well at high altitude except for an unfortunate tendency to inflate like a balloon, restricting a pilot's movements and pressing the visor painfully into the face.

Kammler issued a new specification for a rigid suit and concealed it within a Navy requirement for a deep-diving suit for salvage teams. This project resulted in the *Schwerenraumanzug* (SRA) heavy space suit, which featured metal joints and an armored helmet.

Developments of the SRA were reportedly in use as late as the 1970s. *Kampfrüstung Siegfried* was a class of power armor developed for heavy

The development of the hardened *Dräger* space suit was hidden within a *Kriegsmarine* requirement for advanced diving gear. (Artwork Hauke Kock)

infantry use as well as construction, and larger versions include the *Kraftbein* heavy-lifting walker.

Operations

The *Walhalla* base's various research, development, and manufacturing projects are described in the next chapter. The base's day-to-day operations are also worthy of mention for the ingenious ways in which the *Walhalla*'s crew overcame the particular challenges of building and maintaining a base on the Moon.

The *Haunebu III* craft were designed with an endurance of seven to eight weeks, about seven times the duration of the *Apollo 11* Moon-landing mission in 1969. Performance figures for the *Haunebu IV* are not available, but it can be assumed that its endurance was at least equal to that of its predecessors.

Once on the Moon, though, Kammler and his scientists had to give the problem of sustained life support their most urgent attention.

Air

The *Haunebu* craft were equipped with air recyclers, and captured SS records show that Kammler took at least 40 air recyclers from the Blohm & Voss yards in Hamburg, where the Type XXVI U-Boat was under development. These were designed to sustain a crew of 33 during voyages lasting several weeks, and would have stretched the performance of the *Haunebu* oxygen generators considerably.

Although the specifics of the base's life support equipment remain a mystery, it is clear that Kammler and his followers were able to create a stable, pressurized environment that has kept *Walhalla*'s personnel alive for more than three generations.

Kammler certainly had the personnel and equipment to extract oxygen, hydrogen, and nitrogen from the lunar soil, either by conventional electrochemical means or by using vril power. Electrolytic oxygen-hydrogen reactors would provide auxiliary power and yield drinkable water as a by-product.

NASA's *Surveyor 3* lander on the lunar surface. The *Surveyor* program mapped a great deal of the lunar surface and provided vital reconnaissance data on the moonbase. (NASA)

Water

The waste water recyclers aboard the *Haunebu* craft were designed to sustain each saucer's crew for no more than two months, and the considerably larger population of the *Walhalla* base, as well as the needs of food production, made it vital that Kammler and SS E-IV find ways to extract water from the lunar soil. The oxygen-hydrogen reactors mentioned above produced water as a by-product, but not in sufficient quantities to sustain the colony indefinitely.

Water ice is present in the surface layers of the Moon, in small and localized patches where comets have crashed into the lunar surface and thrown up enough debris to cover the ice before it can sublimate and be dispersed by the solar wind. A photograph taken by the *Luna 13* lander in December 1966 shows what appears to be an abandoned open-cast mine against the southeast wall of the crater where it landed, as well as markings that appear to be tire tracks. The presence of water on the Moon was not confirmed until 2009, but experts believe that the *Luna* chanced upon an ice extraction site in the shadow of the crater wall.

Food

Hydroponics, the science of growing plants without soil, had been developed in the 1930s. One of the earliest successful applications was developed by Pan

The *Walhalla* moonbase was initially made up of components that were shipped from Earth and assembled within the Aristarchus crater.

1. The *Haunebu IV* saucer acted as the command center and provided accommodation for the base's personnel.

2. Eight of the smaller *Haunebu III* saucers were refitted as laboratories and workshops. Their KSK armaments were moved to upper-side mountings and provided the base's defensive firepower.

3. A *Glocke* power source, shipped from a mine in Silesia, provides the base with almost unlimited power.

4. The base is held together by a network of airtight tunnels, improvised from the pressurized fuselage sections of Ta 400 high-altitude bombers.

5. The V-9 rail gun, capable of hurling building-sized rocks at Earth, provided the base's main offensive armament.

OPPOSITE
A view of the moonbase circa 1967, based on classified images from the American *Surveyor* program. The *Haunebu* craft that form the base's primary structures can clearly be seen, along with the *Glocke* power source and the V-9 rail gun. The rim of the Aristarchus crater can be seen on the horizon.

American Airlines on Wake Island. Later to become famous in World War II, this rocky atoll was an important refueling stop for Pan Am's Trans-Pacific flights, and the airline grew fresh vegetables for their passengers when the cost of shipping them in proved prohibitive.

In January 1948, Operation *Windmill* discovered the remains of the abandoned Neuschwaben landbase in Antarctica. Among the remains of the base the expedition's scientists discovered clear evidence of hydroponic cultivation of wheat, rye, and several vegetables, which would have been as vital in Antarctica as it is on the Moon. Geological surveys and lander missions from the 1960s on have confirmed that the lunar surface provides all the minerals necessary to mix a "Hoagland solution" soil substitute.

In addition, biologists attached to Operation *Windmill* recovered bones and droppings that indicated the presence of sheep, pigs, and cattle at the Neuschwaben landbase, as well as laboratory equipment consistent with artificial insemination and genetic research. A classified report in the files of the US Air Force concludes that the fleeing Nazis took any remaining livestock with them.

Waste Processing

In designing the *Walhalla* base, Kammler took every precaution to avoid wasting resources that could not be as readily replenished on the Moon as

THE GLOCKE

Also known as the Yaktavian Bell, the *Glocke* power source developed out of Thule Society research, which indicated that placing mercury under magnetic stress could alter its fundamental nature and release a virtually unlimited supply of energy.

Under the name *Lanternenträger* (Lantern-Bearer), a project was begun in fall 1943 to construct a *Glocke* in Silesia's Wenceslas Mine. Using a radioactive mercury isotope called Xerum 525, the *Glocke* was large enough to power the entire Third Reich, in theory at least.

Russian and Polish forces overran Silesia in 1945. During the early years of the Cold War, it was feared that the Soviet Union had captured the *Glocke* and would turn its power against the United States and its allies. These fears were not allayed until 1968, when *Apollo 8* photographed it in the Aristarchus crater. How it was smuggled out of Germany remains a mystery.

Die Glocke ("the Bell") was moved from Silesia ahead of the Allied advance. Using a radioactive mercury fuel, it remains the main power source for the base. (Murriemir)

they could on Earth. Waste processing begins with water extraction and purification to replenish the base's modest water supply.

Next, the dried waste passes through a number of fermentations which yield methane and other hydrocarbons. These were especially important during the base's early years when certain operations were still fueled by combustion engines, but since the mid-1960s the zero-point energy from the *Glocke* has replaced the need for hydrocarbon fuels. Now, they are used mainly to supplement the soil substitute used in the base's hydroponic labs.

In the final stage, the remaining waste is processed chemically to extract trace amounts of various metals and minerals. Based on US experiments over the last decade, it is estimated that less than 0.18 ounces of non-recoverable waste is produced per person, per day.

Power

After the primary structures of the base were in position, the power plants of the *Haunebu* craft were coupled together to create a working power grid. While this was sufficient for day-to-day operation, Kammler had calculated that a much larger power source would be required in order to meet the needs of the various special projects relocated to the Moon.

As an interim measure while the *Glocke* zero-point energy source was being set up, the saucers' power plants were supplemented by a steam-turbine system improvised from stripped U-boat parts. An array of water-filled pipes took advantage of the Moon's daytime surface temperatures of around 240 degrees Fahrenheit to generate electricity. Never intended to last, this makeshift system failed after a few months under the extreme stress of lunar temperature variation: without the moderating effects of an atmosphere, day and night temperatures can vary by as much as 400 degrees Fahrenheit.

Once the *Glocke* was online, the steam turbine system was largely cannibalized for parts and raw materials. However, as late as 1958 an early Soviet *Luna* mission photographed what seemed to be a scrap yard containing lengths of pipe and partial turbine blades.

Communications

As part of the Bifrost Protocol, the *Haunebu IV* was fitted with a Würzburg-Riese *Gigant* radar system with a range of over 60 miles. The system has been continually upgraded over the years, and according to classified US Air Force documents the base was able to detect an attacking MQ-37 drone from a range of 200 miles during a 2015 mission. The Würzburg array is supplemented by various radio and television antennae which allow the base to monitor transmissions from Earth.

A *Würzburg-Reise* radar dish. Normally ground-based, a unit was fitted to the *Haunebu IV* craft. (MoRsE)

Outgoing radio traffic from the *Walhalla* base was first detected by Britain's Jodrell Bank Observatory in early 1949. The first radio intercepts were handed off to the Government Code and Cipher School at RAF Eastcote in west London, which found that they were internal base communications and not, as was first suspected, messages to surviving Nazis on Earth. The watching brief passed to a joint project run by GCHQ from its Cheltenham headquarters with assistance from MI5 and the Ministry of Defence. By 1951 both the CIA and KGB had become aware of the lunar transmissions and set up their own monitoring programs; these led directly to the US and Soviet space programs, which are discussed in a later chapter.

Resource Extraction

Under the Bifrost Protocol, Kammler planned to take enough resources to the Moon to sustain the *Walhalla* base for the first three months of its life. During that period, all personnel not directly involved in base construction were assigned to lunar exploration and prospecting. These early missions showed that iron, oxygen, and silicon were comparatively abundant on the lunar surface, along with magnesium, aluminum, manganese, and titanium. As expected, carbon and nitrogen were extremely scarce, and a stringent waste recycling program was set up to preserve what had been brought from Earth.

Metal extraction and refining became one of the most important day-to-day operations as soon as the *Glocke* power source was working. A number of linear and squared-off features have been photographed on the Moon, contrasting markedly with the craters surrounding them. Some have been claimed as proof of alien activity on the Moon, but while NASA and other government agencies have declined to comment beyond condemning the photos as fakes, a few writers have noted that these images are similar to aerial photographs of open-cast mines and their supporting road networks.

Moonbase Projects

When Kammler devised the Bifrost Protocol, he had more in mind than simply the survival of Nazi ideology and advanced technology. He knew that removing vital projects and personnel to the Moon would buy a window of time in which the *Walhalla* base would be undetected, and a longer window within which the Allies would be unable to reach it – and he intended to make full use of that time.

Kammler applied stringent criteria in selecting the projects that would be taken to *Walhalla*. Some were necessary for the survival and development of the base itself. Others had to offer a way to strike back during the base's period of impunity, or a means of returning to Earth in force when the time was right. All had to be feasible in the harsh and airless lunar environment.

The operations of the *Walhalla* base were organized into four divisions, or *Abteilungen*, covering life population, weapons, space flight, and support. Every project was assigned to the appropriate division.

The Divisions

Life Support Systems, including construction and maintenance (*Abteilung für Lebenserhaltungssysteme*): The most important of the divisions when *Walhalla* was founded, this division has settled into a maintenance role.

Weaponry (*Abteilung für Geschütze*): This division oversees all long-range weaponry, and is in charge of *Projekt Mjölnir*.

Spaceship Development, Production, and Operation (*Abteilung für Weltraumfahrzeuge*): This division is in charge of *Walhalla*'s saucer fleet, and plays a major role in long-range defense missions to Earth, and the preparations for *Projekt Gungnir*.

Population and Personnel (*Abteilung für Bevölkerungswesen*): In addition to running the base's *Lebensborn* program, this division oversees technical and troop training as well as the development of metahuman personnel and, a little strangely, the android program, *Projekt Eisenmann*.

Lebensborn

The Division for Population and Personnel was tasked with ensuring that the base's population could sustain itself over as many generations as necessary until the Bifrost Protocol was completed. As well as maintaining a sufficient population to provide for the base's personnel needs, this division took charge of political indoctrination, education, and training.

The *Lebensborn* program was begun by the SS in 1935 with the goal of finding children who possessed the physical characteristics of the Aryan ideal to increase the breeding stock of the Aryan race. Initially the project focused on SS members and their families, but as the war progressed it became common to seize children from occupied countries and bring them to Germany for "re-education."

Although the *Lebensborn* program did not come directly under Kammler's command, by 1945 his prestige within the SS enabled him to requisition more than 200 *Lebensborn* aged 13–18 for "technical apprenticeships." Apprentices were selected for their devotion to Nazi ideals as well as for technical aptitude. This younger population was the seed of a self-sustaining community that would keep the base staffed over a period of generations, as plans and preparations were made for a return to Earth and the creation of a new Nazi Reich.

Lebensborn Mutants

The small gene pool within the *Walhalla* base significantly increased the odds of mutations arising within the *Lebensborn* population. A few very heavily-built figures have been seen on surveillance images of the base, and after-action reports from the 1972 American assault mentioned a few so-called "Trolls," of massive build but lower than average intelligence, formed into four-man *Sturmtruppe* sections and used as an expendable, berserker-style shock force for base defense.

The Myth of Hitler's Brain

There have been persistent rumors that Hitler's brain was smuggled out of Germany before the surrender, and that it may exist somewhere in a cloned body or even an armored robot. The *Walhalla* base is one possibility, but most intelligence analysts and experienced Nazi-hunters consider it a remote one.

There are two main theories regarding the whereabouts of Hitler's brain. At least some of his body was smuggled to Brazil where Josef Mengele planned to create cloned copies of the Führer. This plan was Mengele's own, and was thwarted in 1978 by a Viennese Nazi-hunter. Rumors that Hitler's brain was taken to a separate location in South America have never been proven.

The second theory arose after an American secret agent reported encountering a power-armored Hitler in a remote German castle where various other experiments were taking place. The report was initially dismissed because Hitler was known to be in Berlin at the time, but a similar encounter was reported in Romania in 1952. Some writers now believe that a clone of Hitler – or of his head – was encased in a robotic body and removed either to the Moon or to the center of the Earth.

At the time of writing the truth of the matter is unclear, although it cannot be denied that a resurrected Hitler would have a powerful symbolic value for a planned Nazi return to Earth.

The limited gene pool at the base led to a higher than normal incidence of mutation, including individuals with great strength but limited intelligence. (Artwork Hauke Kock)

Eisenmänner

Especially during its initial construction, the *Walhalla* base had a great need for workers able to operate in the airless lunar environment. Space suits were available for a few key workers, but much of the heavy work was relegated to heavy androids known as *Eisenmänner* (Iron Men). Over time, the *Eisenmänner* were developed into two separate classes, one for heavy construction tasks and another for battle.

The battle robots mount two 20mm KSK weapons in place of arms and are reported to be capable of moving at 50mph in a series of kangaroo-like hops. In 1972, more US casualties were attributed to these robots than to enemy ground troops or fixed defensive weaponry. Recent surveillance images have shown similar figures estimated to be 12–15 feet in height, although it is not certain whether these are a new, larger generation of robots or manned, powered battlesuits developed from the same basic design.

Mensch-Maschinen

Between the death of Stalin in 1953 and the Cuban Missile Crisis of 1962, rising tensions between the United States and the Soviet Union led to a real possibility of nuclear war. It has long been rumored that, in addition to the functionally-designed *Eisenmänner*, German scientists were working on a class of *Mensch-Maschinen* (Man- or Human Machines): perfect androids that could pass for normal humans – and even for specific individuals.

There are some who believe that *Mensch-Maschinen* were actually deployed on Earth during this period. The CIA and the KGB both investigated claims that certain prominent individuals – among them US Senator Joseph McCarthy and Soviet leader Nikita Khrushchev – were diverted from important meetings and replaced by *Mensch-Maschinen* whose mission was to raise Cold War tensions to the point where the two superpowers wiped each other out. If this could be accomplished, it is argued, the final phase of the Bifrost Protocol could be put into effect. The Black Sun fleet could return to Earth and found its Fourth Reich on the ruins of Europe and North America.

Although its proponents point out various incidents during this period when prominent leaders on either side seemed bent on provoking a nuclear exchange, this theory remains controversial. Both governments continue to deny that their leaders were anything other than themselves at this time, while a rival theory proposes that their instability was caused by Nazi agents using some kind of mind-control weapon.

Base Defenses

Although *Walhalla* was untouchable when it was first founded, the Order of the Black Sun knew that this could not last. Therefore, a high priority was given to base defenses. Initially, the KSK weapons from the *Haunebu* saucers were moved from the crafts' undersides to improvised top mounts, but further development has taken place ever since.

Energy-Beam Weapons

In addition to the saucers' KSK armament, Kammler brought a number of other weapon projects to the Moon, with the intention of developing them in parallel until a clear front-runner emerged.

The *Feuerball* electrostatic weapon was the first to be dropped: it was soon discovered that outside the protection of the Earth's magnetosphere, the Solar Wind and other sources of radiation interfered catastrophically with its

A captured *Kraftstrahlkanone* turret displayed in a Russian museum. The KSK was the most successful of several energy-beam weapon projects. (Artwork Hauke Kock)

guidance systems, and its electrostatic output was too small to have any effect on a craft that was hardened against the levels of radiation that are common on the Moon.

The *Kugelblitz* fell by the wayside almost as quickly, and for the same reasons. Research focused on the three energy-beam weapon projects: Rheotron, *Röntgenkanone*, and the combat-tested KSK. Over time, the *Rheotron* and *Röntgenkanone* projects merged to produce a viable long-range weapon: continually developed and upgraded, the KSK has remained *Walhalla*'s main defensive armament.

Reconnaissance before the US attack in 1972 found that large KSK weapons – ranging from 20–80mm – had been mounted to give clear fields of fire upon every part of the base's surroundings, with outposts on the rim of the Aristarchus crater. These emplacements remain today – doubtless with upgraded weaponry – and so far they have been the main targets of recent American MQ-14 drone strikes.

Another area of development has been in the field of laser weapons. The *Eisenmänner* battle robots are armed with powerful lasers, and in 1972 US troops also encountered Nazi troopers armed with rifle-sized versions.

Missiles

By 1944, Germany was developing a number of guided and unguided missiles. In addition to strategic bombardment weapons like the V-1 and V-2, a number of promising surface-to-air missiles (SAM) and air-to-air weapons were being designed to help break up American bomber boxes, and so were radio-controlled antishipping missiles.

By February 6, 1945, Kammler had canceled all SAM projects, intending to divert personnel and resources to *Haunebu* and KSK development. However, he did take a number of Hs 117 *Schmetterling* and Reinmetall-Borsig *Reintochter* missiles to Antarctica as defenses for the stopgap Neuschwaben landbase. American aircraft did not come within range of these weapons during Operation *High Jump*, and they were never used. American forces who explored the base during Operation *Windmill* found them abandoned, apparently because their control surfaces, designed for use in Earth's atmosphere, made them useless on the Moon.

However, Kammler did take a number of unguided rockets with him to bolster *Walhalla*'s defenses. The *Werfer-Granate 21* was unpopular with the Luftwaffe because of the drag caused by its wide launch tube, and Kammler had little difficulty acquiring a stock of these weapons, which he mounted in modified *Nebelwerfer* multiple launchers. An upgraded version of the same system was encountered by US forces in 1972. The rockets created dense clouds of flak that were capable of shredding an unarmored space suit, with catastrophic consequences for the wearer.

Recent US drone missions have not encountered any flak defenses. Military analysts believe that all the base's rockets were expended in 1972 and never replaced, either because the ingredients for their fuel and warheads are hard to find on the Moon, or because of the base's increased reliance on KSKs and other energy-beam weapons.

A *Werfer-Granate 21* rocket being loaded onto a Focke-Wulf Fw 194 fighter. Luftwaffe pilots disliked the drag caused by the launch tubes, but this weapon proved very effective during Operation *Lyre*. (Bundesarchiv Bild 101I-674-7772-13A)

Long-Range Weapons

To carry out the second phase of the Bifrost Protocol, Kammler needed long-range heavy weapons capable of bombarding Earth from outside its atmosphere. Von Braun had made sure that Germany's rocket research was out of his grasp, but he had access to several other weapons, both existing and in development.

The Weaponry Division had to solve three main problems before the *Mjölnir* phase of the protocol could begin. First, all weapons, along with any ammunition, had to be fabricated largely from resources that were available on the Moon, and be capable of operating in lunar conditions. This meant that they could not rely on conventional propellants like cordite or gunpowder.

Second, the projectiles themselves had to be large enough to survive entry into the Earth's atmosphere without burning up completely. This meant they had to be at least 33 feet in diameter, or about the size of a house. In all of history, no artillery piece had ever been designed with a caliber over 914mm, less than one-tenth the required diameter.

Finally, several targeting problems had to be overcome. Any Moon-to-Earth weapon would have to be mounted in a fixed emplacement because of its size, using the relative motion of the Earth and Moon to come to bear on a target. Since a projectile would take more than a day to reach the Earth, firing required complex calculations. Even then, the shot could be deflected by the atmosphere, striking off-target, burning up at high altitude, or even bouncing back out into space.

The V-9 Rail Gun

The Allies had put paid to the V-3 emplacements in France before they could become effective, but in 1945 the design represented Germany's best hope for developing super-long-range artillery. A larger version of the gun was built between 1949 and 1950 to fire non-explosive lunar rocks of about 440 pounds. Its size was dictated by the limitations of using explosive charges in lunar conditions and the projectiles usually broke up in the upper layers of Earth's atmosphere.

However, from 1949 to 1954 a handful of them traced a line across Russia and Western Europe, although none hit a settlement of any size. The relative motion of the Earth and the Moon, and in particular the Earth's rotation, made targeting a complex process, especially in the east–west dimension. These difficulties are evident from the fact that out of seven impacts along a corridor measuring less than 100 miles from north to south, none fell within 200 miles of a capital city or any other significant target.

Dissatisfied with the results of the first weapon, Kammler ordered a complete redesign. The new weapon, designated V-9, employed the same long-barreled, fixed design but was a rail gun, using electromagnetic energy from the *Glocke* to fire rocks as large as a two-story house, that were better able to survive entry into Earth's atmosphere. At the same time targeting calculations were improved to take better account of the deflection caused by impact on the upper atmosphere.

The V-9 performed better than the V-8, but not by much. Between 1965 and 1992 a handful of "meteors" fell within 20–40 miles of London and New York, causing minor damage.

Some commentators have claimed that the spectacular Chelyabinsk event of 2013 was a test firing of an improved V-9. The meteor – if that is what it was – has been estimated as being about 66 feet in diameter and weighing

THE V-3 GUN

While the *Vergeltungswaffen* (Vengeance Weapons) program is best known for the V-1 cruise missile and the V-2 ballistic missile, it produced plans for weapons of many other types. Among the few actually built was the V-3 "supergun," a 150mm cannon intended to bombard London from sites in occupied France.

The V-3 consisted of a long, fixed barrel set on a ramp or hillside. Multiple side-chambers were arranged along the length of the barrel, containing secondary charges (or, later, rocket boosters) which increased the speed of the projectile as it passed by. The smoothbore weapon fired a fin-stabilized 150mm shell with a range of around 100 miles.

Two V-3 sites in the Pas-de-Calais region were knocked out by Allied bombers before they could fire a shot; two other sites bombarded Luxembourg from December 1944 to February 1945 before being overrun by advancing Allied troops.

more than 13,000 tons when it struck the outer atmosphere. While both Russian and US intelligence sources publicly state that it was a natural event, there are rumors that it was really the first shot fired by an enlarged version of the V-9 gun, which has been tentatively designated V-10.

However, the fact that it struck some 1,500 miles east of Moscow and even further from any other large Russian city is thought to indicate that targeting problems have yet to be fully overcome. Nazi Germany had not developed any significant level of computer science by 1945, and analysts believe that the *Walhalla* base is still reliant on analog technology for long-range targeting calculations.

The Oberth *Sonnengewehr*

In 1929, the German physicist Hermann Oberth developed the idea of constructing a 330-foot wide concave mirror in Earth orbit. The curvature of the mirror would allow it to focus the sun's rays on a single point on the Earth's surface, creating enough localized heat to burn a city. Initially it was dismissed as science fiction, but Kammler took up Oberth's idea and set up a secret research facility at the village of Hillersleben in Saxony to develop the *Sonnengewehr*, or "Sun Gun."

Although no effective results had been achieved by the end of the war, captured German scientists claimed that the weapon was only five to ten years from completion. One major hurdle was the project's reliance on the unfinished A-12 rocket to lift the components into orbit: it has been estimated that several hundred A-12 missions would have been needed to complete the mirror and its control mechanism. The July 23, 1945 issue of *Life* magazine carried an illustrated article on the mirror, including many details of its proposed construction.

The V-3 cannon was prevented from bombarding London as Kammler had planned, but a larger version was built at the base to launch projectiles at the Earth. (Bundesarchiv Bild 146-1981-147-30A)

Kammler initially developed the *Sonnengewehr* in parallel with the V-8 and V-9 guns, but after their disappointing performance the mirror project took on a higher priority. Instead of being constructed in space, the *Sonnengewehr* would occupy a crater, using the relative movement of Earth and Moon as a crude aiming mechanism just as the guns had done. Building on the lunar surface simplified construction considerably, and Kammler knew it would take the Allies much longer to reach the lunar surface than to achieve Earth orbit, giving the weapon a longer operational life.

The *Sonnengewehr* has a significant advantage over projectile weapons such as the V-9 because its beam of concentrated light can reach the Earth in under two seconds, compared to almost three days for a V-9 projectile. This simplifies targeting significantly, allowing a shot to be aimed using open sights without the need for complex calculations. However, it requires a precise alignment between Sun, Moon, and Earth, making its effective firing windows both narrow and infrequent.

The GSK

In 2009, surveillance images showed a very large turreted emplacement under construction near the northwestern rim of the Aristarchus crater. Detailed analysis of enhanced images led to the conclusion that the mount was designed to hold a very large, single-barrel weapon which could cover the whole of the Earth.

At first, it was thought that the weapon would be an improved V-9 rail gun – perhaps even the V-10 that had long been predicted – but further study concluded that such a weapon would be too large for a turret mount to be practical, even in the Moon's lower gravity. Instead, it seemed that the Black Sun was building a long-range energy-beam weapon capable of reaching the Earth.

Such a weapon – dubbed "GSK" (*Grosse Kraftstrahlkanone*) after the smaller weapons used for base defense – would not have the Sonnengewehr's restricted firing windows or the V-9's complex targeting calculations. Powered by a *Glocke* buried deep under its emplacement, it could be brought to bear on any city-sized target on Earth using an optical telescope, and fired at will.

Although details of the recent American drone campaign against *Walhalla* are highly classified, it seems likely that the threat of the GSK – a true Nazi "death ray" every bit as deadly as its comic-book precursors – led directly to the development of the MQ-14 Lunar Hawk drone and its deployment against *Walhalla*. If the GSK were ever to become operational, it would turn the Moon into a literal "death star" and allow the Order of the Black Sun to dictate terms to every nation on Earth – or to complete Nazi vengeance against Germany's former enemies and return to rule the world.

Nuclear Weapons

Nazi Germany lagged behind the Allies – and particularly the United States –

OPPOSITE
While inspired by the V-3 supergun, the V-9 rail gun was substantially different in operation as well as size. Redesigned for lunar conditions, it used electromagnetic propulsion rather than explosive charges to hurl building-sized rocks at the Earth. Its performance proved disappointing, however: most of its projectiles either burned up in Earth's atmosphere or missed their targets due to computational errors.

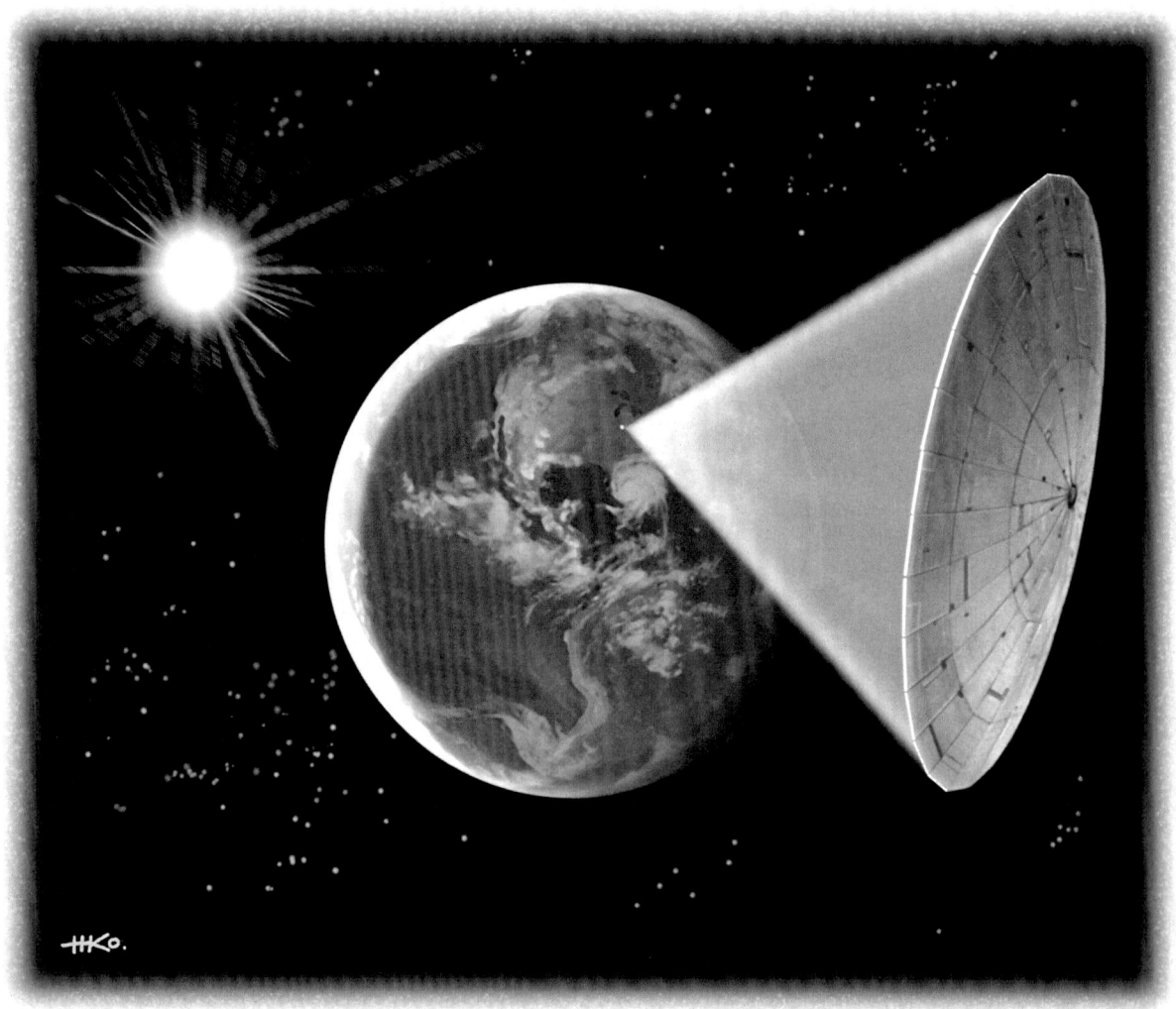

The Oberth *Sonnengewehr* was not constructed in orbit as originally planned, but a larger version, constructed on the Moon, was tested during the late 1940s. (Artwork Hauke Kock)

in the development of nuclear weapons. When the Nazi Party came to power in 1933, nuclear physics was one of several branches of research that were vilified as "Jewish science." Einstein, who was visiting America at the time, did not return to Germany, and many other physicists and mathematicians left the country over the following years. After the invasion of Poland, many of those who remained were drafted into the army. It was not until 1942 that Germany truly began to take nuclear weapons development seriously.

SS E-IV removed as much nuclear research as it could from the experimental site at Haigerloch on the edge of the Black Forest, leaving behind one experimental nuclear pile and a handful of scientists who were captured by American forces. It had been planned to develop a nuclear warhead for the V-2, and for the planned A9/A10 "America Rocket," but when Kammler activated the Bifrost Protocol, the warheads were far in the future and the rockets themselves had been lost when von Braun escaped into American hands with many of his key scientists.

The Black Sun has made many attempts to capture an American or Russian nuclear warhead for study. As early as December 1948, UFO activity was reported over American bases that housed nuclear weapons, and this pattern has continued to the present day. While no warheads have been confirmed as missing, it is regarded as an open secret that multiple covert missions have been launched from the *Walhalla* base with the object of recovering American or Russian nuclear materials and research. So far, there has been no attempt to launch nuclear weapons at Earth from the Moon, but most analysts are unwilling to discount the possibility that the base does have such weapons.

Spaceship Development

Reports and images of UFO sightings since 1947 show that Black Sun engineers have developed three distinct generations of saucer craft from the *Haunebu* design.

The first generation, in service roughly from 1947 to 1955, had an angular profile with a vertical-sided central command structure and three or four hemispherical blisters on the underside. UFOlogists refer to this design as the "Adamski" type after George Adamski, who published photographs and accounts of contact with "Nordic aliens" in the early 1950s.

From the later 1950s to the mid-1970s, this saucer design evolved into a more streamlined shape, presumably to improve in-atmosphere performance. The central structure became more spherical, and the saucer profile became smoother overall. Bell-shaped at first, the saucers developed a symmetrical profile as the saucer element was moved up to the midline of the cabin.

Since the later 1980s, a third generation of spacecraft has been sighted with increasing frequency. No longer a saucer shape, these "black triangles" have been seen across Europe and North America. At first, military authorities dismissed reports as sightings of the then-secret B-2 stealth bomber, which was not shown to the public until 1988; however, most black triangles were much larger and capable of hovering and other flight maneuvers that a B-2 could not replicate.

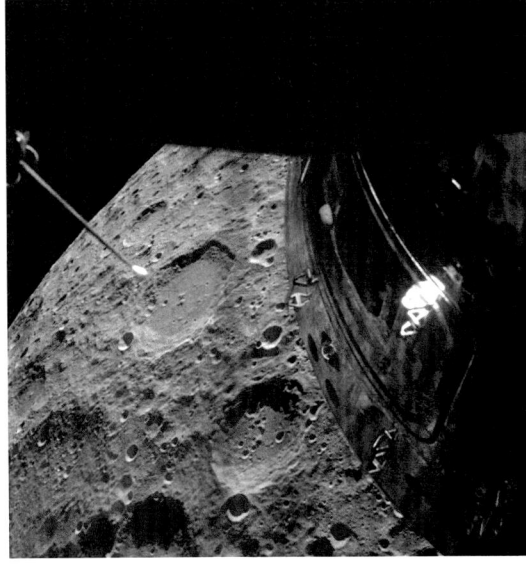

A shot of the moon as from the *Apollo 13* Lunar Module. (NASA)

This type now seems to be the most common ship coming from the *Walhalla* base. It has been estimated that a typical craft, approximately 330 feet long, could accommodate up to 5,000 assault troops and their equipment. So far, the black triangle missions have been non-aggressive, apparently scouting locations or testing Earth's responses, but some experts believe that American actions on the Moon have prompted the Order of the Black Sun to abandon the *Mjölnir* bombardment phase of the Bifrost Protocol and initiate preparations for the planned *Gungnir* invasion.

The Hunt for the Moonbase

> "I believe that this nation should commit itself to achieving the goal, before this decade is out, of landing a man on the Moon and returning him safely to the Earth. No single space project in this period will be more impressive to mankind, or more important for the long-range exploration of space."
>
> President John F. Kennedy, May 25, 1961

By the time President Kennedy gave his famous speech committing the United States to a Moon landing, both the US and the Soviet Union had been engaged in secret efforts to reach the Moon for over a decade. Although Cold War rivalry was certainly a factor in the so-called "Moon Race," it was not the only one: by now both powers knew that the *Walhalla* base existed, and that it both posed a threat and offered a treasure trove of advanced technology to whichever of the two superpowers could reach it first.

Early Satellites

Although both superpowers had captured enough documents and parts to give them a fragmentary picture of Nazi saucer research, neither one had enough information to replicate it. Initial experiments at Area 51 had led to a worldwide UFO scare in the late 1940s, but had not yielded a viable craft. Soviet engineers, meanwhile, had been unable to develop a craft capable of leaving the ground.

Both powers recognized the necessity of developing a space-flight capacity quickly. Each knew its rival was using captured German scientists to develop the dreaded V-2 into an intercontinental ballistic missile capable of delivering a nuclear warhead, which would enable it to project its power across the globe. By 1947, each power also knew that the most dangerous Nazi technology had been removed from Earth to somewhere in space, where it posed a continuing threat despite the fall of Nazi Germany. For the time being, rocket technology was the only avenue by which either superpower could pursue the goals of space travel and global nuclear domination.

At first, it was thought the Nazis were building a space station in Earth orbit. Plans for the Oberth *Sonnengewehr* had been recovered by Allied intelligence, and captured German scientists had boasted that the project had

John F. Kennedy and Nikita Khrushchev. Cold War rivalries were stoked by the determination of both superpowers to capture and gain the secrets of Nazi superscience. (Keystone Pictures USA / Alamy Stock Photo)

been only five years from completion by war's end. A massive survey of Earth's immediate surroundings ensued, involving optical and radio telescopes and culminating in early orbital missions from the *Sputnik* and *Pioneer* satellite programs to the manned *Vostok* and Project *Mercury* orbital missions, but nothing was found.

Project *A119*

Project *A119* was begun in 1958 by the US Air Force. Its plan was to detonate a nuclear warhead on the Moon "for scientific purposes," as well as to boost morale in the face of the Soviet Union's early lead in the space race. According to recently declassified documents, however, this was a thin cover story for the destruction of the Nazi base in order to keep its secrets out of Soviet hands if they should reach the Moon first.

The project was canceled in January 1959, however, after calculations revealed that the largest warhead the United States could then place on the Moon was 1.7 kilotons, about 10 percent of the yield of the Hiroshima bomb. Given the margin of error in targeting a nuclear weapon over such a distance, it became obvious that such a small explosion did not guarantee the destruction of the base, even if its presence in the Aristarchus crater could be confirmed.

Project *Moon-Blink*

Project *Moon-Blink* was a collaborative lunar survey launched by NASA in 1964, after it became apparent that the rumored Nazi space base was not

The US *Lunar Orbiter* program provided the first high-quality reconnaissance photographs of the base. The images themselves are still classified. (NASA)

orbiting the Earth. Its aim was to study so-called Transient Lunar Phenomena (TLPs) which had been reported with increasing frequency over the previous 15 years. From 1949 onward, flares of light, often blue or purple in color, had been reported from the Aristarchus crater in the northwest part of the Moon's near side.

Project *Moon-Blink* took thousands of images of Aristarchus and the surrounding area, along with the Alphonsus crater on the southeastern side of the Mare Imbrium where other phenomena had been reported. Although the images were not clear enough to distinguish structures, the project did conclude, in a secret memo to President Lyndon Johnson, that Aristarchus required further investigation.

Lunar Probes

In 1959 the Soviet *Luna 2* probe missed the Aristarchus crater and landed on the other side of the Mare Imbrium. Other *Luna* missions placed orbiters around the Moon, equipped with cameras to search for signs of human activity.

Meanwhile, the US *Ranger* program had yielded a few images of the lunar surface before its probes crashed, but none showed anything that looked like a moonbase. The *Ranger* program was not an unqualified success. *Ranger 1* and *Ranger 2* failed to launch; *Ranger 3* to *Ranger 5* all failed in flight, with two missing the Moon completely; and *Ranger 6* suffered a camera failure that may have been due to a hit from a *Röntgenkanone* or similar weapon. Improved shielding on the last three *Ranger* probes allowed them to transmit detailed images back to Earth, but their usefulness was limited by the fact that they were designed to crash into the lunar surface.

The *Lunar Orbiter* program of 1966–67 was more successful: in five missions it mapped 99 percent of the Moon's surface with a resolution of 200 feet or better, and provided confirmation of man-made structures in the Aristarchus crater.

This information was used in planning the *Surveyor* series of landers, which transmitted clearer images of the *Walhalla* base before landing in widely scattered locations from June 1966 through January 1968. This deliberate dispersal of landing sites had two objectives: to make it harder for Nazi scientists to recover the landers and analyze their technology; and to preserve, if possible, the illusion that they were part of an innocent scientific mission by a United States that had no idea of the *Walhalla* base's existence.

In regard to the second objective, at least, the strategy was a failure: spies inside von Braun's staff at NASA were already feeding information to *Walhalla*, keeping the Black Sun fully informed about American progress on the hunt for the moonbase. Information leaked by these agents enabled *Walhalla* to shoot down *Surveyor 2* and *Surveyor 4* without American knowledge: from the NASA control center, the effects of a KSK hit were impossible to distinguish from a malfunction in the landers' propulsion systems.

Manned Lunar Missions

While the American Moon program was conducted openly after Kennedy's pronouncement in 1961, its Soviet counterpart was kept secret, and its existence was even denied. The Russians did not want their rivals to know how close they were to launching a manned Moon mission: their thinking was that the Americans would not rush so long as they thought they were ahead, giving the Soviet Union time to develop superior technology. Also,

Apollo 12 astronaut Charles Conrad examines the *Surveyor 3* probe to recover untransmitted images. This mission may have spurred *Walhalla*'s commanders to attack *Apollo 13* and shoot down later unmanned probes. (NASA)

The *Lunex* lander design inspired both the Space Shuttle and the Lunar Hawk attack drone. (PD)

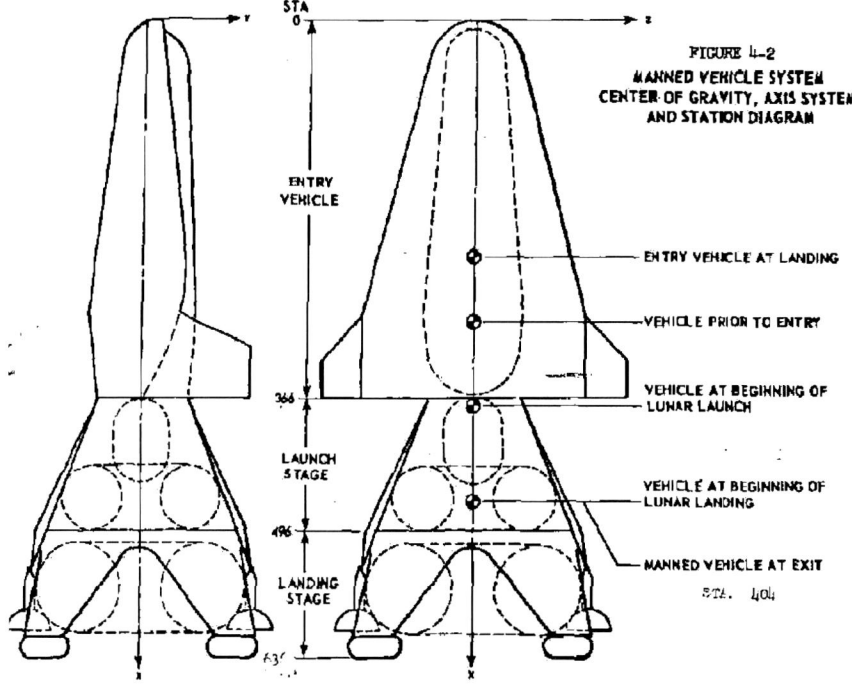

according to documents declassified in the *glasnost* era of the 1980s, it was felt that by openly declaring their progress in the Moon Race the Americans made themselves a more prominent target for any Nazi reprisals.

The whole world watched when astronaut Neil Armstrong stepped onto the Moon in 1969, but the heart of the *Apollo 11* mission was taking place 60 nautical miles above, where Michael Collins, in the command module *Columbia*, was continuing the reconnaissance work undertaken by previous *Apollo* missions to photograph the *Walhalla* base. Since *Apollo 8* had first orbited the Moon in late December of 1968, NASA had photographed the base with ever more powerful cameras to assess its defensive capabilities. Back on Earth, planning experts analyzed the photographs and film brought back from the *Apollo* orbiters and developed an assault strategy.

While the *Apollo* missions were putting boots on the ground and developing expertise for a planned ground assault, the Russian plan took a different approach. The *Zond* series of missions are still described as planned Moon landings, but they secretly aimed to create an orbiting base assembled from *Soyuz 7K-L1* components, which would be used to knock out the *Walhalla* base's defenses from long range before dropping troops to conquer it. As will be seen, though, this plan did not reach completion.

US and Soviet Moonbases

In parallel with their early satellite programs, the United States and the Soviet Union both began planning moonbases of their own, with the intention of taking the war to the Moon and extinguishing the Nazi threat once and for all.

APOLLO 13

The Black Sun response to the *Apollo* landings came in 1970 with the attack on *Apollo 13*. When the spacecraft came within five and a half hours of lunar orbit, it was struck by a KSK energy beam that caused an oxygen tank to explode, severely damaging the Service Module and causing the mission to be aborted.

For three tense days, the world watched as the crew struggled to survive and return to Earth in their crippled spacecraft, believing American press releases that wrote the explosion off as an accident. In American military circles, though, it was well known that this was an attack, and a response was urgently needed.

Apollo 13 was the last of the program actually to be launched. The remaining four missions were simulated in the Nevada desert while the United States secretly switched its efforts to developing von Braun's proposed moonbase in order to mount an assault on *Walhalla* and end the Nazi threat once and for all.

The effort was also spurred by growing Cold War tensions: whoever controlled the Moon, it was thought, would also control the Earth.

Lunex and Horizon

In 1958–59, both the US Army and US Air Force commissioned plans to establish a manned base on the Moon by the mid-1960s.

Project *Lunex,* the Air Force plan, used a one-piece lander and return vehicle that looked something like the Space Shuttle of the late 20th century. It planned to establish a permanent American presence on the Moon by 1968. Officially, the project was scrapped over crew safety concerns, and because the lander would require an even larger rocket than the Saturn V to take it to the Moon. However, various aspects of the Lunex designs were developed as classified projects at the famed Lockheed-Martin "Skunk Works" and saw service as components of Project Horizon.

Project *Horizon* was conceived by Wernher von Braun's team at the Army Ballistic Missile Agency, and aimed to establish a manned moonbase by 1967. Saturn-A boosters would be used to lift components into orbit, where they would be assembled at a space station. The project was examined at the highest levels, and then shelved in favor of the *Apollo* program.

After the attack on *Apollo 13*, however, priorities changed. After a total of 40 classified launches in 1970, the so-called "lunar shuttle" was complete, and starting in January 1971 it landed structural components on the southwestern edge of the Mare Imbrium, a comfortable distance from the *Walhalla* base. A defensive perimeter was set up immediately, consisting of low-yield *Davy Crockett* nuclear rockets and Claymore mines adapted to

This NASA photograph shows damage to *Apollo 13*'s service module, probably resulting from a long-range KSK hit. (NASA)

The Strategic Defense Initiative was aimed at defending the United States against Nazi spacecraft as well as Soviet missiles. (PD)

pierce space suits. The first phase of construction was complete by April and over the following 18 months a large complement of trained volunteers from every elite branch of the US military was secretly moved in.

Zvezda and Zond

The Soviet *Zvezda* project was begun in 1972. It was planned to deliver prefabricated modules to the Moon using the N1 rocket, Russia's answer to the Saturn V, and assemble the base on the lunar surface. This plan had the advantage of creating a base that could be made operational far more quickly than its American counterpart. However, the project suffered serious delays because of the problematic N-1, and after 1970 the plan was abandoned in favor of the *Zond* orbital station. Having observed the failure of Operation *Lyre* in 1972, however, the plan was canceled in 1974 without a shot being fired.

Operation *Lyre*

Operation *Lyre* took place on March 17–19, 1972. Over 200 specially-trained US troops moved overland from the *Horizon* base, assaulting *Walhalla* on the morning of March 19. The attack was the culmination of a plan that had begun six months earlier: an initial rocket attack aimed to knock out the base's heavier defenses while ground troops in modified space suits conducted a ground assault.

The attack was a complete failure. Although the initial rocket barrage did some damage to *Walhalla*'s heavier defensive weaponry, lighter point-defense weapons wrought terrible havoc among the Americans, who were forced back three times before abandoning the attack. Details of the mission are still classified, and the casualties were hidden within the military losses for the First Battle of Quảng Trị which began on March 30.

The main effects of Operation *Lyre* were to knock out the *Sonnengewehr* and cause minor damage to the V-9 rail gun. Some called this a partial success, although neither weapon had yet been able to cause serious damage on Earth. However, it undoubtedly had an effect on the Black Sun's decision to abandon *Projekt Mjölnir* and accelerate plans for the next phase of the Bifrost Protocol.

With the failure of Operation *Lyre*, the Horizon base was abandoned and the survivors were shuttled back to Earth. The Apollo program was wound down: two more missions were flown, but the pretense was no longer necessary: the United States had abandoned the Moon.

In the Soviet Union, military planners considered their options. Work on the *Zond* project was still hampered by flaws in the N1 rocket system, and despite the damage to two of *Walhalla*'s long-range weapons a Nazi reprisal attack was feared. For the next two decades, both superpowers switched their priority from attacking the Moon to defending the Earth.

Orbital Defenses

After Operation *Lyre*, the technological advantage switched back to the Soviet Union. It already had a working orbital station thanks to the *Salyut* program, while the United States was forced to catch up with the *Skylab* project. Through the later 1970s and the 1980s, orbital stations of increasing sophistication served to provide early warning of approaching threats and, if necessary, direct ground-launched missiles to their targets.

The *Salyut* Program

Building on the *Zvezda* concept, the Soviet Union already had advanced plans for space station construction as early as 1971. *Salyut 1* was launched in April of that year, and had been intended as a dry run for the construction of the planned lunar orbital station when the failure of Operation *Lyre* made both superpowers rethink their strategy. Russia's *Almaz* program aimed to create a series of military space stations using *Salyut* technology, but after three missions it was decided to focus instead on automated defense satellites coordinated from a single manned station. This project continued under the *Almaz* name through the later *Salyut* missions of the early 1980s and the construction of the *Mir* station. *Salyut 7*, the last of the series, remained in orbit until 1991.

Although several moonbase projects have been proposed since 1972, the continuing threat from *Walhalla* has led to a focus on unmanned missions. (NASA)

63

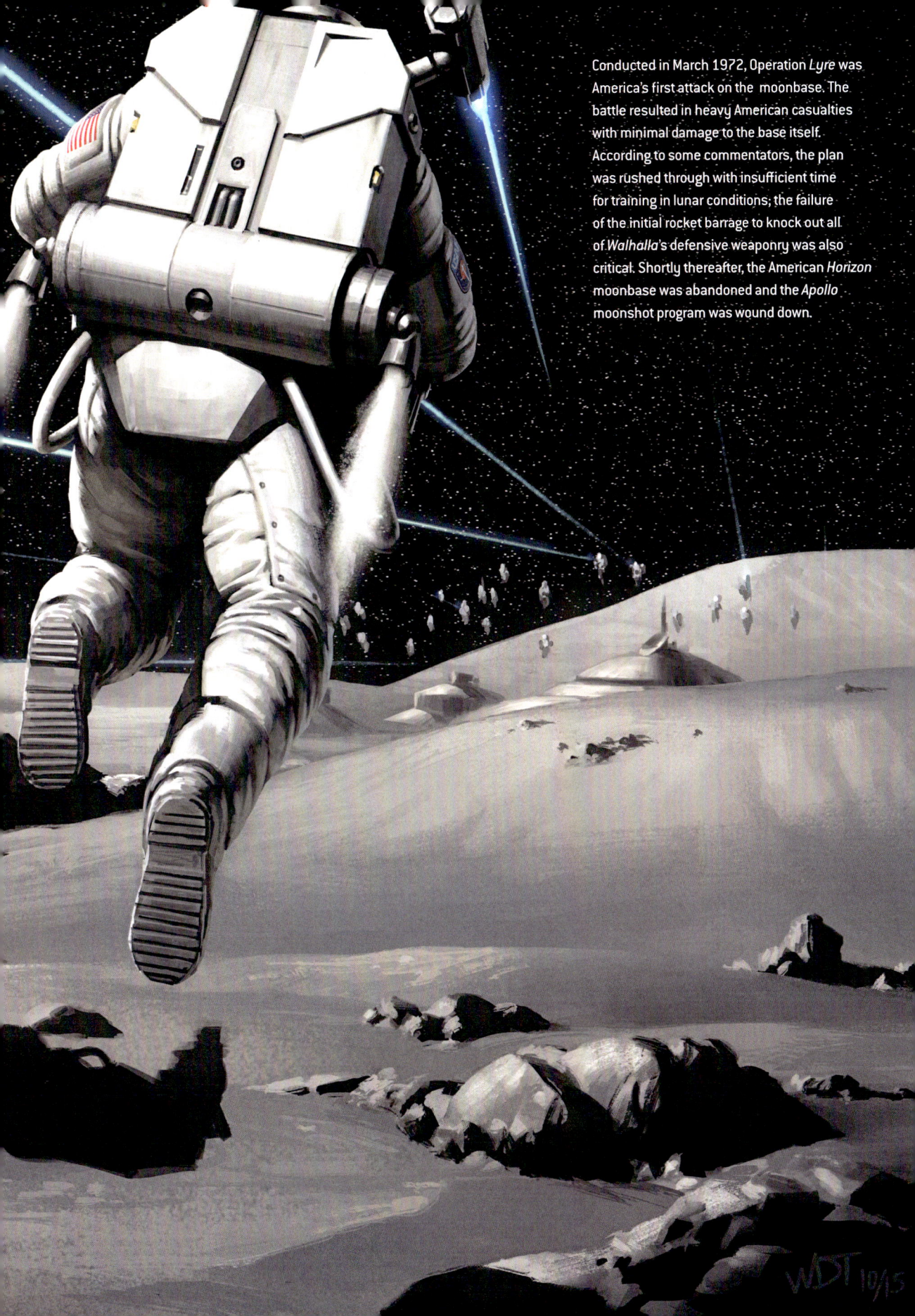

Conducted in March 1972, Operation *Lyre* was America's first attack on the moonbase. The battle resulted in heavy American casualties with minimal damage to the base itself. According to some commentators, the plan was rushed through with insufficient time for training in lunar conditions; the failure of the initial rocket barrage to knock out all of *Walhalla*'s defensive weaponry was also critical. Shortly thereafter, the American *Horizon* moonbase was abandoned and the *Apollo* moonshot program was wound down.

Skylab

Barely a year after Operation *Lyre*, NASA launched *Skylab I*, an orbiting scientific station whose stated purpose was to make astronomical observations, survey the Earth from space, and conduct experiments in zero gravity. It also had a classified mission: to detect approaching spacecraft and direct the fire of ground-launched missiles. This mission was largely carried out by automated systems, allowing *Skylab* to work continuously between the three manned missions to the station. Upgrades to Skylab's detection and communications systems continued throughout its lifetime, and there was a plan to use the Space Shuttle to boost it to a higher orbit, but delays in Shuttle development prevented this operation from taking place. *Skylab* finally dropped out of orbit on July 11, 1979, breaking up on re-entry. The largest pieces came down near Perth in Western Australia.

Killer Satellites

The Soviet military had developed the *Istrebitel Sputnik* (IS; Fighter Satellite) concept in the 1960s as part of the *Zond* project, which saw the orbiting moonbase as the command and control center for a fleet of attack satellites parked in lunar orbit. Like the *Zond* space station, it was a simple matter to adapt the system for use in Earth orbit, both looking outward for approaching Nazi craft and looking out for rival US satellites.

Upon detecting an enemy launch from the lunar surface, the *Zond* command module would direct the nearest IS satellite toward it: the satellite would detonate a fragmentation warhead which was effective at a range of up to half a mile.

Until 1983, US orbital defense relied on missiles launched from the Earth's surface. That year, however, President Ronald Reagan launched the Strategic Defense Initiative (SDI). Nicknamed "Star Wars," this ambitious program surrounded the Earth with a network of satellites armed with X-ray lasers and rail guns. The project was sold to the public as a defense against Soviet intercontinental ballistic missiles, raising Cold War tensions to a pitch not seen since the Cuban Missile Crisis, but equally important was its ability to detect and destroy incoming Nazi saucers.

The launch of the first SDI satellites led to a brief period of orbital dueling to accompany the political and military posturing on the Earth's surface. Although Soviet Premier Yuri Andropov publicly declared an end to the IS program, US and Soviet satellites continued to spar with each other until the collapse of the Soviet Union.

ASAT Missiles

In addition to orbital stations and armed satellites, both superpowers relied on conventional missiles to bolster their defenses against an attack from space. Known in military circles as ASATs, antisatellite weapon programs were usually piggybacked onto antiballistic missile (ABM) development, frequently using the same launch vehicles.

Initial development stalled in the 1960s when the electromagnetic pulse from a nuclear ASAT caused disruption across a wide area of the Pacific, but after 1972 ASAT development assumed a new urgency with Earth thrown onto a defensive footing. Since that time several countries have developed an ASAT capability, most notably China, India, and Israel, which arguably has the most to fear from a Nazi attack on Earth.

The 1980s and Beyond

The collapse of the Soviet Union severely disrupted the Russian space program, although several Soviet initiatives continued. The *Mir* space station remained operational, and the SH-11 "Gorgon" ABM was deployed around Moscow along with other defenses such as the 53T6 "Gazelle" system.

In the United States, the lander from Project *Horizon* developed into the Space Shuttle, which was instrumental in deploying a network of military and civilian satellites that covered the entire globe. According to leaked Department of Defense documents, the satellites of the Global Positioning System (GPS) include a classified module codenamed SID (Space Intruder Detector) that watches for incoming threats including missiles, asteroids – and presumably, though this is never openly stated, Nazi saucers. The SID system is patched into the secret network of SDI hunter-killer satellites, and controlled both from the ground and from the International Space Station.

The International Space Station

Launched in 1998 and expanded several times, the International Space Station (ISS) began as a US/Russian cooperation after the *Skylab* and *Mir* stations became obsolete. The European, Canadian, and Japanese Space Agencies have also contributed modules, and astronauts from several other countries have served tours of duty aboard.

In addition to its scientific work, the ISS continues to serve as the primary command and control center for Earth's orbital defenses. Each member nation also maintains a backup control center: Houston, Texas; Baikonur, Kazakhstan; Kourou, French Guiana; Saint-Hubert, Quebec; Tanegashima, Japan; and Harwell, England.

Recent Moon Shots

In 2004, President George W. Bush proposed an American moonbase by 2020, but the idea quickly evaporated after initial cost estimates. Some observers believe that Bush wanted to capitalize on the early success of Operation *Iraqi Freedom* and bring the war against *Walhalla* into the open; others claim that the almost instant dismissal of the project was part of a cover-up organized by the US military and intelligence communities after Bush accidentally

An MQ-14 Lunar Hawk attack drone awaiting servicing after a mission. (NASA)

OPPOSITE

The MQ-14 Lunar Hawk drone developed from the X-37 unmanned spaceplane, and is the primary weapon of Operation *Eclipse*. Drone strikes against the moonbase commenced in May 2015 and are ongoing at the time of publication. All details of the operation remain classified, although a squad-carrying X-37 variant is said to be in development, perhaps for a mop-up operation after the drone-strike program is completed.

came perilously close to exposing the existence of *Walhalla*, which has been classified Above Top Secret for almost 70 years.

Since 1990, more nations have joined in the effort to monitor the *Walhalla* base and protect the Earth from future attacks. Results have varied.

In 1990 the Japanese *Hagoromo* orbiter was quickly neutralized, despite a highly elliptical orbit that left it vulnerable only during brief passes. Its transmitter was knocked out, probably by a *Röntgenkanone* or *Kugelblitz*-derived weapon. In 2007 the SELENE project placed three satellites in elliptical orbits around the Moon, transmitting data back to the Tanegashima Space Center. Despite heavier shielding than the *Hagoromo*, the SELENE mission's *Kayuga* main orbiter crashed into the lunar surface in 2009 after suffering control problems. The *Okina* relay satellite was brought down a few days later. A similar fate was suffered by the European Space Agency's *SMART-1* orbiter in 2006 after three years of observations, and India's *Chandrayaan-1* probe after just ten months. These three shootdowns, of small satellites (3.5–5 feet each side) at distances of 60 miles or more, have led some commentators to express dismay at the frightening precision of *Walhalla*'s long-range defensive weapons; others suggest that all were lucky shots, finally hitting their targets after months of trying.

In 2007, China launched its own Moon probe, *Chang'e 1*. About four times the size of *Okina* and *SMART-1*, it was brought down 15 months after entering lunar orbit. The *Chang'e 2* remained in lunar orbit for nine months before leaving the Moon for other objectives, and seems to have escaped unscathed.

In December 2013, the *Chang'e 3* lander touched down across the Mare Imbrium from *Walhalla* and deployed the *Yutu* rover. At some time during

the next lunar night (December 26–January 11), however, the rover suffered unspecified mechanical damage and has been unable to move since, stranded less than 165 feet from the lander. It is uncertain whether the damage is coincidental, as the China National Space Administration claims, or whether *Yutu* was intentionally immobilized by scouts sent from *Walhalla* to investigate the lander. The launch dates for the *Chang'e 4* and *Chang'e 5* missions have since been postponed from 2015 and 2017 to "before 2020."

Meanwhile, Russia's planned *Luna-Glob* project aims to put more rovers on the Moon, perhaps for reconnaissance purposes. Although *Yutu* was disabled within a few days of landing, some schools of thought believe that a small, fast-moving rover, able to take advantage of ground cover, may be able to recover more information at closer range than an orbiter.

Operation *Eclipse*

The X-37 unmanned space-plane flew its first test mission in April 2010. Almost immediately, the US Air Force ordered a modified version, known as the X-37B. In a classified program, this was developed into the MQ-14 Lunar Hawk, a drone attack vehicle.

Emboldened by the success of drone strikes as a strategy in the War on Terror, the US Air Force began developing a secret lunar drone strategy in 2008. The first attack on *Walhalla* took place at 4pm Eastern Standard Time (10pm Central European Time) on May 8, 2015: 70 years to the minute from the signing of Germany's unconditional surrender in Berlin.

Like the military drones deployed in the Earth's atmosphere, the MQ-14's small size and agility make it harder to detect and target than an orbiting satellite or a manned spacecraft. The design incorporates many stealth features that help mask it from enemy radar, and its avionics suite includes an Automated Terrain Following (ATF) package allowing it to fly at extremely low altitudes, making the most of ground cover.

Despite official silence on the matter, rumors have leaked out about "Operation *Eclipse*," a sustained drone bombardment of the *Walhalla* base. Meanwhile, Boeing has announced that the X-37C space-plane will feature a pressurized cargo bay large enough to accommodate six astronauts – the equivalent of an infantry squad and its equipment.

At the time of writing, details are hard to come by. Information is fragmentary and usually denied. However, it is possible that the Operation *Eclipse* drone strikes are intended to strip *Walhalla* of its defensive armament in preparation for an assault which will, at last, lay the ghost of 1972's disastrous attack. It may not be too much longer before the secrets of Nazi superscience are in American hands: what America will do with them remains to be seen.

OPPOSITE
The X-37B unmanned space-plane being prepared for launch inside a faired nosecone. The MQ-14 Lunar Hawk attack drone is launched in an identical manner. (NASA)

Appendix: Timeline

1922 Summer: The vril *Jenseitsflugmaschine* is built, allegedly based on psychic transmissions from Aryans who had been living in the Aldebaran system since 1919.

1934 June: The *Rundflugzeug* (Disk Aircraft) RFZ1 crashes on a test flight at the Arado works in Brandenburg.

1939 Date unknown: First flight of the *Haunebu I* saucer.

1941 Date unknown: First flight of the *Vril-1-Jäger*, the first armed disk aircraft.
December 3: Sänger submits the design for his *Silbervogel* orbital bomber to the Reich Air Ministry.

1942 February 25: The Battle of Los Angeles: US forces fire more than 1,400 antiaircraft rounds at a large UFO without apparent effect.
July 6: The Reich Armaments Ministry reverses its previous policy of dismissing nuclear physics as "Jewish science" and begins Germany's atomic bomb program.

1943 August–September: Flight tests of the BMW *Flügelrad* begin at Prag-Kbley airfield in Czechoslovakia.

1944 Date unknown: Dornier wins the contract to manufacture *Haunebu II* saucers, but production is impeded by Allied bombing. Hans Kammler plans the Bifrost Protocol and arranges the construction of a base on the Moon.
September 8: The first V-2 rockets are fired at Paris and London.
November–December: *Feuerball* electrostatic weapons are deployed against Allied bombers, giving rise to the first reports of "foo fighters."

1945 March: Kammler is promoted to *Obergruppenführer* and placed in charge of all *Wunderwaffen* production.
April: American forces capture the experimental nuclear reactor at Haigerloch near the Black Forest.
April 14: The US Third Army captures the prototype Rheotron accelerator at Burggrub, Bavaria.
April 30: Hitler allegedly commits suicide in Berlin. Rumors of his survival immediately begin to circulate.
May 2: Wernher von Braun surrenders to American troops. His broken arm, sustained while escaping an assassination attempt orchestrated by Kammler, is explained as the result of a car crash.

May 8: VE Day is announced, formally ending the war against Nazi Germany.

Before May 11: The *Haunebu IV* saucer limps out of Prague ahead of the Soviet approach and moves to the Neuschwabenland base in Antarctica.

July 9 and 23: *Time* and *Life* magazines both carry reports on the Oberth "Sun Gun," based on captured documents.

1946 December: Operation *High Jump*: The US task force converges on Antarctica.

1947 February 6: Operation *High Jump*: US forces are repulsed after an air battle with German saucer craft.

March–November: Operation *Einherjar*. The Antarctic base is evacuated and all personnel and other assets are relocated to the Moon. Initial construction of the *Walhalla* base takes place.

June 24: Pilot Kenneth Arnold encounters a crescent-shaped craft near Mount Rainier, Washington, whose movement he describes as "like a saucer if you skip it across water." This is the start of the great UFO scare of the 1940s and 1950s.

July 8: An experimental saucer aircraft from Area 51 crashes on a ranch near Roswell, New Mexico.

1948 January–February: Operation *Windmill*: US forces find the Antarctic base abandoned. The hunt for another Nazi refuge begins.

February 18: A large meteorite falls in Norton County, Kansas, on a similar latitude to New York.

March 25: An Area 51 saucer crashes near Aztec, New Mexico. Rhesus monkey test subjects on board are mistaken for diminutive aliens.

December: Reports begin of UFOs apparently investigating American nuclear facilities and bases where nuclear weapons are stored. These may be Black Sun missions attempting to capture nuclear technology.

1949 Early, date classified: Signals from the *Walhalla* base are first intercepted by Britain's Jodrell Bank radio-telescope observatory.

September 21: A meteorite strikes Beddgelert, Wales, close to the latitude of Birmingham.

1950 September 20: A meteorite strikes Murray, Kentucky, on a latitude close to that of San Francisco.

December 10: A meteorite airburst over St Louis sparks a nuclear attack scare.

1951 October 17: A meteorite strikes near Elenovka, Ukraine, USSR.

1954 March 6: A meteorite strikes Nikolskoye near Moscow, USSR.

November 30: A meteorite strikes a home in Sylacauga, Alabama (on a similar latitude to Los Angeles), injuring one person.

1958 Date unknown: The *Lunex* project plans a US Moon landing in 1967 and an underground moonbase by 1968. It is abandoned in 1961 due to technical difficulties.

May: Project *A119* is begun, planning a nuclear attack on the *Walhalla* base. It is abandoned in January 1959 after calculations show that the United States could not place a sufficiently large warhead on the Moon.

1959 April 7: A meteorite falls near Příbram, Czechoslovakia, about 30 miles from Prague.

June 8: Project *Horizon* proposes a lunar outpost by 1966. Officially, it never progresses beyond a feasibility study and is abandoned in favor of the *Apollo* project. It is revived after the attack on *Apollo 13*.

October 13: A meteorite strikes a house in Hamlet, Indiana, close to Chicago.

1965 April 16: Project *Moon-Blink* begins a survey of the Moon to search for signs of Black Sun activity.

December 24: Meteorite fragments shower Barwell, England, close to Birmingham.

1966 December 24: *Luna 13* lands in the Ocean of Storms, transmitting images to Earth for five days before being disabled.

1967 July 11–15: Meteorites fall on Denver, Colorado, close to the Rocky Flats nuclear weapon facility and the North American Aerospace Defense Command (NORAD) center.

1968 December 24: *Apollo 8* achieves lunar orbit and takes high-resolution photographs of the surface, including the *Walhalla* base.

1969 July 19: *Apollo 11* enters lunar orbit. While Neil Armstrong and Buzz Aldrin land on the Moon, Michael Collins conducts a classified photographic survey of the *Walhalla* base.

1970 April 14: *Apollo 13* is damaged by long-range fire from the *Walhalla* base, forcing the mission to be aborted. The remaining *Apollo* missions are simulated while Operation *Lyre* is planned.

1971 January: The revived Project *Horizon* begins landing components for the creation of an American moonbase.

1972 March 17–19: US forces from Horizon base attack *Walhalla* but are repulsed. Both US and Soviet planners switch their strategy from attack to defense.

1973 March 15: A meteorite falls in San Juan Capistrano, California, close to Los Angeles.

May 28: *Salyut 2* begins the *Almaz* program, aimed at creating a ring of armed Soviet satellites to defend against US intercontinental ballistic missiles and saucers from *Walhalla*.

October 27: A meteorite falls near Canon City, Colorado, close to the NORAD command center and the US Air Force Academy.

1978 February 22: The first GPS satellite is launched as the US aims to counter the Soviet *Almaz* program.

Officially canceled in favor of the *Apollo* program, Project *Horizon* was revived after the attack on *Apollo 13*. (Artwork Hauke Kock)

1980 December 29: First reported sighting of a "black triangle" UFO, near an American air base at Rendlesham Forest in Suffolk, England.

1983 March 23: US President Ronald Reagan announces the Strategic Defense Initiative. Officially this is a response to the Soviet nuclear threat but it is also intended to track and shoot down trespassing Black Sun saucers.

1985 September 13: The US conducts a successful test of the Vought ASM-135 antisatellite missile, launched from an F-15 fighter from 38,100 feet. The ASM program is developed as a backup to SDI satellite defenses in case of a saucer attack from *Walhalla*.

1990 January: The Japanese probe *Hagoromo* loses its transmitter after coming under fire from *Walhalla*, and is unable to transmit any data back to Earth.

1992 October 9: A meteorite falls in Peekskill, just outside New York City.

2006 September 3: The European *SMART-1* probe is shot down.

2009 Date uncertain: Surveillance images show construction of a large turret, possibly for a giant KSK weapon. Dubbed the "GSK," this structure becomes a high-priority target.
March 1: The Chinese *Chang'e 1* probe crashes onto the lunar surface after being fired on by *Walhalla*.
June 10: The Japanese *Kayuga* orbiter crashes into the lunar surface. Officially the crash was planned, but the crash date was brought forward by two months owing to damage from an unspecified source. The *Okina* relay satellite, part of the same Japanese mission, is brought down a few days later.
August 29: Contact with the Indian *Chandrayaan-1* probe is lost, probably as a result of fire from *Walhalla*.

2010 January 18: A meteorite falls in Lorton, Virginia, close to Washington, DC.
April 22: First launch of the X-37 unmanned space vehicle, ancestor of the MQ-14 drone.

2012 April 22: A meteorite explodes above Sutter's Mill, California, not far from San Francisco.

2013 February 15: A huge meteorite, estimated at over 10,000 tons, explodes over Chelyabinsk, Russia.

2014 January 25: China's *Yutu* rover is immobilized a few hundred yards from the *Chang'e 3* lander after suffering unspecified "mechanical damage." Further *Chang'e* missions are postponed.

2015 May 8: Operation *Eclipse* begins with the first MQ-14 Lunar Hawk drone attack on *Walhalla*. Attacks have been ongoing up to the time of writing.

Further Reading, Watching, and Gaming

Books

Farrell, Joseph P., *Reich of the Black Sun* (Adventures Unlimited Press, Kempton, IL, 2005). Provides a broad overview of Nazi weird science, including UFOs and the Antarctic refuge.

Hastings, Robert, *UFOs and Nukes: Extraordinary Encounters at Nuclear Weapons Sites* (Author House, Bloomington, IN, 2008). A painstaking collection of accounts of UFO incidents at American nuclear facilities since 1948.

Heinlein, Robert, *Rocket Ship Galileo* (Del Rey, New York, 1977). Plucky young astronauts travel to the Moon in a home-modified rocket and encounter a secret Nazi moonbase.

Herwig, Dieter and Heinz Rode, *Luftwaffe Secret Projects: Strategic Bombers 1935–45* (Midland Publishing, Earl Shilton, UK, 2000). Covers various advanced aircraft, including designs for the *Amerikabomber* project.

Hite, Kenneth, *The Nazi Occult* (Osprey Publishing, Oxford, 2013). A brief but wide-ranging survey of Nazi occult and weird-science projects.

Myrha, David, *Sänger: Germany's Orbital Rocket Bomber in World War II* (Schiffer Publishing, Atglen, PA, 2002). An account of one ancestor of Nazi Germany's space program.

Nomura, Ted, and Mirando, Justa, *Luftwaffe 1946 Tech Manual* (Antarctic Press, San Antonio, TX, 2006). A companion to the *Luftwaffe 1946* comic series (see below), this book contains information on saucer craft as well as other advanced aircraft.

Scott, Chris, *Hitler's Bomb* (Stein & Day, New York, 1986). A history of German nuclear weapon research, compared to Allied progress on the same front.

Stevens, Henry, *Hitler's Flying Saucers* (Adventures Unlimited Press, Kempton, IL, 2002). A complete source on Nazi disk craft.

Von Braunfels, Ilsa, *Iron Sky: Nazis on the Moon* (MFM Entertainment, Nashville, TN, 2012). A digital short story tie-in to the first *Iron Sky* movie (see below).

Comics

Mignola, Mike, *Hellboy* (Dark Horse Comics, 1993–present). Nazi superscience and occultism form the background of this long-running comic series.

Nomura, Ted, *Luftwaffe 1946 series* (Antarctic Press, San Antonio, TX, 1996–2006). An adventure comic featuring many of Germany's advanced aircraft designs.

Games

DUST (Fantasy Flight Games). This miniatures game features Nazi mecha and other dieselpunk-inspired troops.

Gear Krieg (Dream Pod 9). A line of tabletop games including roleplaying and miniatures-based titles.

GURPS Weird War II (Steve Jackson Games, 2003). A roleplaying game sourcebook featuring Nazi UFOs and other superscience.

Hellboy: The Science of Evil (Konami, 2008). The comic-book hero battles Nazi robots in Romania.

Iron Sky: Invasion (TopWare Interactive, 2012) is based on the movie of the same name (see below) and allows players to fly various Nazi spacecraft.

Rocket Ranger (Cinemaware, 1988). Features the player collecting rocket parts in order to fly to the Moon and shut down Nazi extraction of a mineral called lunarium.

Tannhäuser (Fantasy Flight Games). A Weird War II miniatures game featuring a wide range of Nazi weird science.

Wolfenstein: The New Order (Bethesda Softworks, 2014) features a moonbase level where the player must stop Nazi nuclear research. Other titles in this long-running series feature Nazi zombies and cyborgs, as well as a power-armored Hitler.

Movies and TV

Danger 5 (2012 and 2015). This Australian action-comedy series parodies Nazi superscience and 1960s action shows as it faces its heroes with various Nazi foes, including a giant mech piloted by Hitler himself.

Hellboy (2004). Based on the comic book series, the movie includes Nazi cyborgs and other fantastic foes.

Iron Sky (2012). This cult movie tells of a Nazi invasion of Earth in 2018, launched from a secret moonbase that has remained hidden since 1945.

Iron Sky: The Coming Race (scheduled 2016). Teasers for this sequel feature a Nazi-ruled Hollow Earth and an undead-looking Hitler riding a Tyrannosaurus rex.

Nazis at the Center of the Earth (2012). Another film about a secret Nazi base within the Hollow Earth, this features Nazi zombies and a battle robot controlled by Hitler's head.

Glossary

Aggregat: The codename for the series of ballistic missiles that included the V-2 (designated A4 in the series). The A9 and A10 rockets were intended to be capable of reaching the continental United States.

Amerikabomber: A project to develop an intercontinental bomber capable of delivering a nuclear weapon to the East Coast of the United States.

Bifrost Protocol: The plan to create the *Walhalla* moonbase. Named for the Rainbow Bridge from Norse myth that connected Midgard, the mortal world, to Asgard, the divine realm where Odin's hall of Valhalla was located.

Black Sun: A secret organization within the Nazi Party, dedicated to occultism and advanced technology.

Braun, Wernher von: A leading German rocket scientist who surrendered to US forces and went on to become a driving force in America's space program.

***Feuerball* (Fireball):** An electrostatic weapon fitted to early German saucer aircraft.

***Flügelrad* (Flying Wheel):** An early German disk aircraft, later abandoned for the *Haunebu* and *Vril* series.

***Glocke* (Bell):** A device for generating and manipulating vril energy. It could be used in various ways, including the excavation of large underground spaces and the opening of wormholes in space and time.

GSK: Nickname for a large KSK-type weapon recently thought to be under construction at the *Walhalla* base.

Haunebu: An abbreviation of *Hauneburg-Gerät* (Hauneburg Device) applied to a series of saucer craft. Hauneburg was a fictitious town created by the SS to confuse Allied intelligence agents searching for the saucer facility.

***High Jump*, Operation:** A US Navy task force sent to probe the Neuschwabenland base in late 1946 and early 1947.

***Jenseitsflugmaschine* (Other-world Flight Machine):** The first documented German flying disk, tested between 1932 and 1934.

Kammler, Hans: Head of *Wunderwaffen* production for the SS and the power behind the *Walhalla* project.

KSK (*Kraftstrahlkanone*): A focused energy-beam weapon fitted to most *Haunebu* craft. Usually supplemented with 30mm MK 108 aircraft cannon because of the enormous power drain caused by firing them.

***Lyre*, Operation:** An unsuccessful US attack on the *Walhalla* base that took place in 1972.

Neuschwabenland (New Suebia): A codename for the Antarctic saucer base. Named for the region of Suebia in southwestern Germany.

***Paperclip*, Operation:** A US operation overseen by the Office of Strategic Services in which over 1,500 German scientists and engineers were recovered and moved to the USA. These individuals proved crucial to the American space program.

***Rundflugzeug* (Disk Aircraft):** The second German flying disk project, which developed into the *Vril* series.

***Silbervogel* (Silver Bird):** A rocket-powered bomber concept developed for the *Amerikabomber* project. The wedge-shaped craft was designed to cross the upper atmosphere in a number of "skips" and land in friendly Japanese territory after delivering its payload.

SS E-IV (*SS-Entwicklungstelle* IV): The SS agency headed by Hans Kammler and involved in the development of advanced weaponry.

***Surgeon*, Operation:** A British counterpart to the American Operation *Paperclip* (q.v.).

***Tachyonator*:** An electro-gravitic propulsion system developed by the Thule Society for use in *Haunebu* and other saucer craft.

Thule Society (*Thule Gesellschaft*): An esoteric group that played a large role in early Nazi occultism and may have been one of the ancestors of the Black Sun movement.

***Vergeltungswaffen*:** Literally "Retribution (or Payback) Weapons," often translated as "Vengeance Weapons." A series of advanced weapon projects designed to destroy cities in Britain (and ultimately the United States as well) from Europe. The V-1 cruise missile and the V-2 ballistic missile were the only V-weapons to enter service, but many more were planned.

***Victalen*:** An advanced alloy developed for the skins of *Haunebu* and other saucer craft. Rumored to be an early form of aerogel layered with metal.

***Vril* (aircraft):** Third-generation flying disk aircraft developed by the Vril Society. Despite early successes, the *Vril* series was superseded by the *Haunebu* project.

Vril (energy): First mentioned in Edward Bulwer-Lytton's 1871 novel *The Coming Race*, vril was the name the Nazis gave to the universal energy that combines heat, gravity, and electromagnetism.

Vril Society (*Vril Gesellschaft*): An esoteric group researching vril and claiming psychic contact with an extraterrestrial Aryan civilization.

Waffen-SS: Literally "armed SS," the military branch of the SS organization and the Third Reich's elite troops.

***Walhalla* (Valhalla):** The codename for the Nazi moonbase.

***Wunderwaffen*:** Literally "wonder weapons," this term was applied to a wide range of advanced Nazi technology, including jet aircraft, the V-weapons, and other projects. Hitler hoped that the *Wunderwaffen* could turn the tide of the war back in Germany's favor.